Ghazwa

Manoj Ankush Shinde

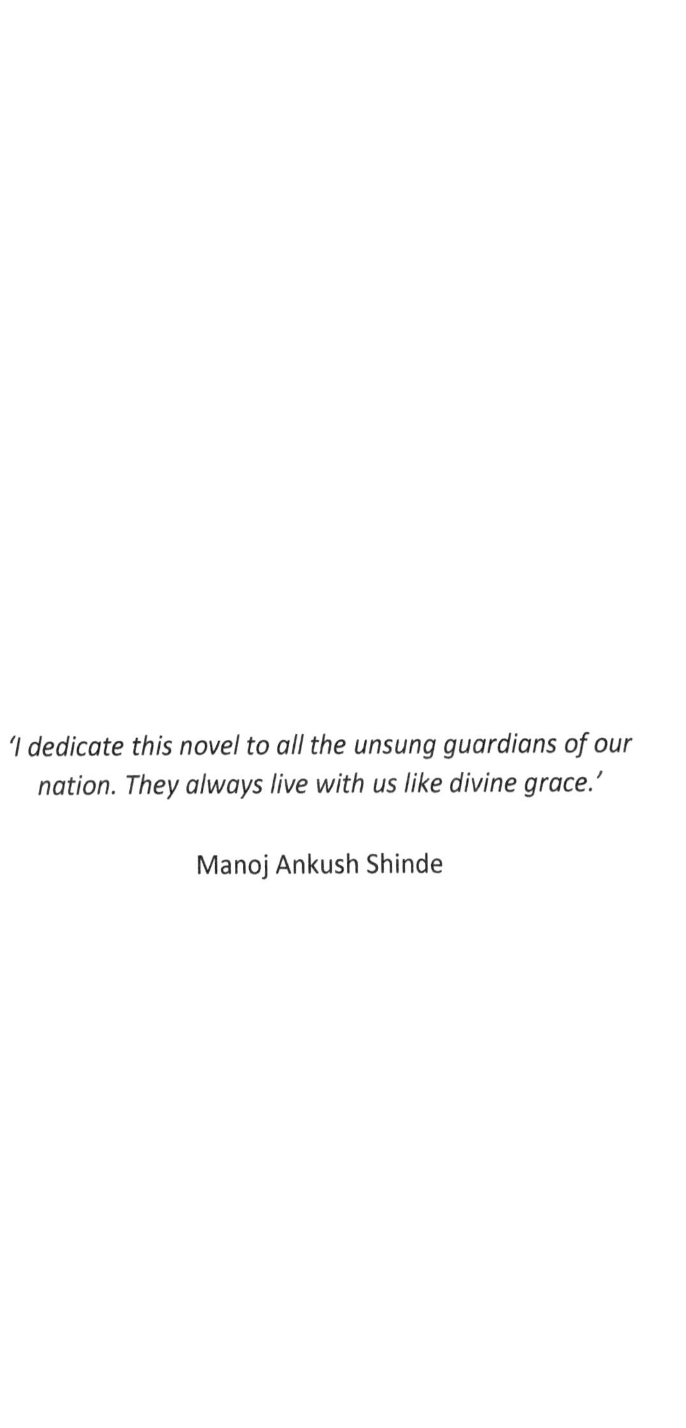

'I dedicate this novel to all the unsung guardians of our nation. They always live with us like divine grace.'

Manoj Ankush Shinde

'Na pecheed mu-ye na ranjeed tan
Ki berun khud aawurd dushman shikan.'

'Thus guided by God himself
And protected by His grace,
He emerges, unscathed, unharmed,
From the enemy's foul embrace.'

Shri Guru Gobind Singh ji Maharaj
Zafarnama

Kokane Chowk.
Pimpri. India.

It is raining heavily. An isolated, abandoned, and dilapidated bungalow hides behind the bushy, muddy compound wall of a massive construction site. There is no water supply, no electricity inside the bungalow. No one is supposed to live there. Yet, for the past four months, two mute boys working at the nearby Al-Hind Biryani Shop have found shelter in its decaying walls. People watch them pass by daily, but their poor instinct bade them not to interfere with poor, hard-working, mute boys.

The throbbing sounds of metal slaying metal, metal drilling stones, and furious cranes lifting and shifting unbearable weight, and a wilderness of thorny weeds and bushes has turned the bungalow into a forgotten grave. An ambulance with mud-stuck tires stands quietly in a bungalow backyard bush like a forced laborer waiting for orders.

The thundering rain drenches the bungalow from outside, a relentless downpour hammering against the walls. Inside, the bungalow has transformed into a macabre Buzkashi court. Carcasses of skinned goats hang lifelessly from the walls, a grim reminder of what has just taken place. Ajmal Khan, a 25-year-old Pakistani law graduate, and Iqbal Badami, a highly motivated 24-year-old IED expert and medical graduate, work with frantic precision. After slaying and skinning the goats, they are now hurriedly stuffing the carcasses with improvised explosive devices (IEDs), their faces focused, their hands moving quickly as they prepare for what is to come.

A stolen car battery powers the lone flickering bulb and charges several mobile phones. In one corner, a few water jars and half-eaten Biryani packets lie dejectedly. The blood-covered floor silently reflects the steady drip from the leaking roof above. Closed doors and sealed windows trap the thick, suffocating stink within the bungalow, letting nothing escape into the outside world of kafirs (infidels).

A *nasheed* plays softly on a Chinese mobile phone, keeping the boys awake for the past six days. The thought of killing infidels and the promise of Jannat's heavenly rewards fuels their resolve for the upcoming fedayeen attack planned in the heart of Pune city. The coordinates of the target have yet to arrive, but their readiness is unwavering. The bungalow is the only place where they speak to each other. Outside, for the rest of the world, they remain completely mute, silent shadows awaiting their moment.

'नमाज़ के बाद सब अपने अपने घर जाकर जिंदगी जीने में मशरूख हो जाते है. कोई हमारी तरह फ़ना नहीं होना चाहता. कोई जिहाद नहीं करना चाहता. उनकी रुहें जन्नत की रूहानियत को महसूस ही नहीं कर पा रही है. और फिर कहते है अल्लाह नाराज़ है,' said Ajmal. Though the fine delicate embroidery on his kurta is *Balochi,* his accent is Peshawari. *After the namaz, everyone goes back and embraces life. No one wants to die like us. No one is interested in Jihad. Their souls cannot see the divine Jannat. And then they say Allah is angry.*

Both know that every passing moment brings them closer to death. Ajmal's nervous fingers stitch the goat's stomach with a thin nylon wire, his hands trembling slightly. He wears a faded brown long kurta and short white pajamas, now stained from the blood. Thick surma around his eyes smudges and mixes with the sweat dripping down his mustache-less, long-bearded face. The scent of his Pakistani Khalis Oudi Attar has long been overpowered by the stench filling the room. His black rubber loafers squelch under a large pile of intestines, livers, and kidneys from the slaughtered goats.

'उन सबको काफिरों के कदमों में मरना है. कब उठेंगे? कब अपनी आंख खोलेंगे? और कब हमारे रास्ते चलेंगे ये लोग? भाईजान कब?' Ajmal added. *They all want to die at the feet of infidels. When will they wake up? When will they open their eyes? And when will they take our path? Brother when?*

A chilling shiver runs through Ajmal's voice as the thought of suicide begins to sink deeper into his mind. His eyes shrink with dread, and sweat beads on his face. Iqbal, however, remains calm, his emotions steady, allowing Ajmal to vent his pent-up frustration without interruption. He listens in silence, his own resolve unshaken, while Ajmal wrestles with the growing fear inside him.

'कब तक हम यहाँ बैठे रहेंगे? कब तक ये सुखी बिरयानी खाएंगे?' asked Ajmal. *How long are we going to wait? How long are we going to eat this stale Biryani?*

'काफिरों के इस शहर ए इक़्तेदार में सब्र. सिर्फ सब्र ही काम आएगा हमे. الله مع الصابرين,' said Iqbal. Like the tiny *Phulkari* embroidery on his *kurta*, his accent is also *Lahori. Only patience will help us in this land of infidels. Allah is with those who are patient.*

Iqbal methodically stuffs the brick-sized wired RDX packets inside the goats, his movements precise and practiced. Ajmal, beside him, continues stitching the goats' skins, his fingers working quickly as he connects the wires threading through the carcasses. The room is filled with the quiet sounds of their grim task, each man absorbed in his role.

The nasheed stops abruptly, and the mobile beeps twice. Ajmal quickly grabs it, his hands shaking slightly as he reads the message. It displays "Red Fort" in Arabic — a code for 'Motibaug, RSS Head Office, Pune.' His eyes shrink with fear, and his heart rattles in his chest.

'भाईजान मोतीबाग. भाईजान इस वक़्त मोतीबाग के रास्ते में भीड़ हो सकती है. यहां से जल्दी निकलना होगा हमें,' said frightened and equally excited Ajmal, rubbing his blood-stained hand to the *pajama. It's Motibaug. We might get traffic. Brother, we must leave now.*

'हमें हुकुम का इंतज़ार करना होगा,' said Iqbal. *We must wait for the final order.*

'वो समझ जायेगा. अब रुकने से क्या फायदा?' asked Ajmal. *He is your elder brother. He will understand. What is point in waiting?*

'अपने जज़्बातों को काबू में रखों अजमल. हम इंतज़ार करेंगे,' Iqbal advised. *Don't be excited Ajmal. We will wait.*

Phone rings. It is Hakimullah on the other side.

'हां भाईजान,' answered Iqbal. *Yes brother.*

'कैसा है छोटे?' asked Hakimullah. *How are you? my little brother.*

'अल्लाह का शूकर है भाईजान,' answered Iqbal. *I am good, brother.*

'स्पीकर पे डालो।' ordered Hakimullah. *Put it on the speaker.*

Iqbal immediately turns the speaker on.

'स्पीकर पे है भाईजान,' said Iqbal. *It is on the speaker brother.*

'हो गयी तैयारी?' asked Hakimullah. *Are you both ready?*

'हां भाईजान सब तैयारी हो गयी,' said Iqbal. *We are ready, brother.*

'अजमल जन्नत में मिलेंगे,' said Hakimullah. *Ajmal we will meet in heaven.*

'इंशाल्लाह जन्नत में मिलेंगे भाईजान,' answered Ajmal. *We will meet in heaven, brother.*

'अल्लाह तुम्हारे साथ है,' said Hakimullah. *Allah is with you.*

'इंशाल्लाह भाईजान,' said Ajmal and Iqbal. *Inshallah, brother.*

'इंशाल्लाह. बारकल्लाहु फ़ीक,' said Hakimullah. *Inshallah. May Allah be with you.*

'बारकल्लाहु फ़ीक्,' greeted Ajmal and Iqbal. *May Allah bless you.*

Ajmal and Iqbal rush the ambulance packed with stuffed goats through the narrow road amid piles of construction material, the tires squealing as they hit the main road. The engine grinds under the weight, but no one stops them. No one suspects their Sikh attire or questions the hospital ID cards flashing around their necks. Iqbal, in the driver's seat, considers taking the Jagtap Dairy route but instinct keeps him on the familiar Nashik Phata road, easing his nerves with the practiced path. Ajmal, sitting tensely in the front seat, mumbles a prayer under his breath, his eyes scanning the passing cars, bikes, footpaths, buildings, and bus stops, searching for any sign of danger. Suddenly, the threat appears in the form of police barricades. The ambulance slows down, tension rising.

'भाईजान?' said Ajamal, pulling his pistol. *Brother?*

'ट्रैफिक पुलिस है. अभी हतियार बाहर मत निकालना,' said Iqbal, slowing down behind the cars. *He is traffic police. Keep the weapon down.*

The police barricade, looming through the heavy rain, instantly sparks deep suspicion. Ajmal's eyes freeze, wearing a thousand-mile stare, unable to look away from the approaching cop. His heart pounds as the officer gets closer, each step amplifying the tension. He sits rigid, fear seizing him, unable to tear his gaze from the threat moving toward them.

'भाईजान ये ट्रैफिक पुलिसवाला नहीं लग रहा,' said Ajmal. *Brother, he is not looking like a traffic police.*

Iqbal's eyes work hard to maintain an air of calm, masking the rising tension. The rain beats down harder as the police officer steps forward and stands directly in front of the ambulance.

'बाहर आ जाओ,' shouted cop. *Come out.*

At this moment, Iqbal clearly senses the looming danger, his instincts screaming at him. Yet, his unwavering faith in the mission holds him steady, delaying any impulse to rush or panic.

'वहां देखो. सब लोग गाडीयों से बाहर निकल रहे है. जल्दी से बाहर आजाओ,' said the cop. *See there. Everybody is coming out. Come on.*

Ajmal's fear trickles down from his temples.

'भाईजान कुछ गड़बड़ है,' said Ajamal. *Brother, something is wrong.*

There is more fear than conviction in Ajmal's trembling voice, but it's enough to convince Iqbal. Instinctively, they both reach for their AK-47s. Just as they begin to lift the weapons toward the cop—BOOM! BOOM! Two bullets simultaneously shatter the windshield and rip through their chests, rupturing their hearts in an instant. BOOM! BOOM! Two more shots from the cop's pistol finish them off, their bodies slumping lifelessly in their seats. Hakimullah's deadly plan to create havoc in India is abruptly foiled.

***

Jamia Naeemia Madrasa

Lahore. Pakistan.

Everything inside this white-bleached campus is cloaked in shadow. At the entrance stands a high-ceilinged, gloomy hall where nearly five hundred boys, aged six to twelve, sit in rows. They rock back and forth in unison, their voices rising together as they loudly recite the Quran.

'السلام عليكم,' greeted Hakimullah to a skinny guard standing at the tall wrought-iron gate and entered the main building. *Salam Walekum.*

Hakimullah, clean-shaven with a flaky, bruised face and medium-length hair, wears a simple polo shirt. In his early thirties, his posture shows signs of fatigue, yet his devotion to jihad remains unwavering. His mission: to eliminate intrigue, idolatry, and infidelity from the world. Behind the name Hakimullah lies Omar Khalid Khorasani, a man steeped in violence and extremism. He played a pivotal role in organizing the infamous Peshawar School Attack, recruiting one Chechen, two Arabs, and two Afghan militants. Their brutal assault claimed the lives of 149 people, including 132 innocent schoolchildren, leaving a scar on Pakistani history.

When the Pakistani army announced the death of Omar Khalid Khorasani, the mastermind behind the Peshawar School Massacre, claiming he was killed in a drone strike in eastern Afghanistan, the world believed the chapter had closed. However, Omar Khalid was far from finished. Shedding his old identity, he continued his operations under a new name—Hakimullah. Unfazed by the announcement of his death, he pressed forward with his extremist agenda, determined to carry out more attacks and evade capture, his presence now even more elusive and dangerous.

Hakimullah quietly navigates through the sea of children reciting in the hall, his presence unnoticed. He slips into the long, dim, arched corridor, where the walls are adorned with colorful English alphabets. But here, the letters tell a different story—J for Jihad, M for Mujahideen—each accompanied by hand-drawn diagrams that detail the working mechanisms of an AK-47 and a bazooka.

The corridor's eerie quiet is broken only by the distant echo of the children's recitations. At the end of the corridor, two athletic men stand guard outside a classroom door, their medium-length beards without mustaches, dressed in olive green salwar-kameez and skull caps. Their gray sports shoes hint at readiness, their hands steady on their weapons as they silently acknowledge Hakimullah's approach.

Nodding to the guards, Hakimullah pushes open the heavy door and steps into the room.

The room is dimly lit, with only a small, closed window letting in a faint sliver of light. Dust and cobwebs cling to every surface, while piles of textbook bundles and broken chairs crowd the space, filling the air with the musty scent of wet wood, rusty metal, and the acrid stench of stale mouse urine. In one corner, three dangerous-looking men with oily faces, thick beards, and skull caps sit cross-legged on a threadbare carpet, their eyes fixed on a flickering video of a busy Indian street playing on a TV set. As the door creaks open and Hakimullah enters, they rise to greet him in unison.

Morad and Hasan, recruits from the infamous and radicalized Lal Masjid in Islamabad, stand with their comrade Mokhtar, their gazes filled with reverence. Their eyes lock onto Hakimullah with deep attention and affection, awaiting his word. The sound of honking cars, bustling crowds, and street vendors continues to echo from the TV set.

Morad, Hakimullah's younger brother, and Hasan, his cousin, stand with unwavering loyalty beside Mokhtar Belmokhtar, the tallest and brightest in the group. Mokhtar, in his early thirties, with a mesomorph build, clean-shaven face, and a student haircut, wears his usual maroon t-shirt. His commanding presence fills the room as he stands as the leader of the Youth Wing of Teherik-e-Khilafa Pakistan (TTK).

Ten years ago, Mokhtar's life was irreversibly shattered when his two-year-old son died in his lap from hunger, diarrhea, and vomiting during the devastating floods in Sindh province. The high waters had already claimed the rest of his family, leaving him alone in a nation where the chronically corrupt public system had turned its back on him. That tragedy fuels the bitterness and fire within him.

In those desperate times, when the world had abandoned Mokhtar, Hakimullah's Teherik-e-Khilafa (TTK) found him. They offered him free food, shelter, and clothes, extending a lifeline when no one else would. This act of support during his darkest hour forged Mokhtar's deep loyalty to the group, pulling him into the fold of TTK's mission.

After joining Lahore College with the help of TTK, Mokhtar's organizational skills quickly set him apart. Within a year, he was entrusted with managing and distributing funds to vulnerable youths across the city. His innovative approach of distributing funds in installments rather than lump sums allowed TTK to stretch its resources and reach more young people. These small yet impactful initiatives brought Mokhtar even closer to Hakimullah, earning him a place among his most trusted men.

Sitting cross-legged on the carpet, all four men—Hakimullah, Mokhtar, Morad, and Hasan—watch the footage. The screen shows a bustling crowd of on of the largest Pandals in Pimple Saudagar, Pune. Children tug at their mothers' hands, begging them to buy balloons from a nearby vendor. An elderly couple negotiates the price of a Pooja-Thali with a flower seller. Nearby, a group of boys and girls dressed in traditional Maharashtrian attire energetically plays Dhol-Tasha. A police patrol van inches through the thick crowd, struggling to move.

An older man, with a long orange beard and wearing a skull cap, sells peacock feathers to a newly married couple, while people walk through a metal detector installed at the Pandal's entrance. The camera catches a large Ganpati idol, draped in traditional Maharashtrian jewelry and vibrant garlands, visible from the entrance. Beside the idol is a diorama depicting Flight Lieutenant Abhinandan with his MIG-21, a symbol of pride and patriotism. The video cuts off abruptly, leaving the room in a tense silence.

Hakimullah, visibly impressed by his team's achievement, rises from the carpet with a quiet sense of approval.

'मोख़्तार बेलमोख़्तार। मोख़्तार बेलमोख़्तार। शुक्रान जज़ीरा। अपनी जान की बाज़ी लगा दी तुमने इस काम के लिए। यहाँ तो सबने तुम्हारे हिंदुस्तान से ज़िंदा वापस आने की उम्मीद छोड़ दी थी। अल्लाह तुम्हारे साथ है। और हां, इतने कम वक़्त में पुने जैसे शहर में लड़कों के रेहने का इंतज़ाम करने के लिए बोहोत शुक्रिया।' said Hakimullah to Mokhtar. *Mokhtar Belmokhtar, Mokhtar Belmokhtar, you risked your life to get us all this. This is great. None of us believed that you would return alive from Hindustan. Allah is with you. Thank you for helping boys in getting shelter in Pune on such a short notice.*

'पुने में हमारे PFY का साथी है. जर्मन बेकरी में काम किया था उसने। लड़के उसी के घर में रुके है,' said Mokhtar. *Our PFY associate of Pune helped us in finding the house and signing rent agreement. He was there in German bakery blast.*

'मसाला फैक्ट्री कहा शुरू की है?' asked Hakimullah about the training center. *Where is the Masala factory?*

'बम्बई से थोड़ा दूर एक पुराना ढाबा है. पुणे हाईवे पर. उसका मालिक बॉलीवुड का प्रोड्यूसर है. गाडी, रहना , खाना सब उसीने दिया।' said Mokhtar. *Away from Mumbai, there is an old dhaba on Pune – Sambhaji Nagar Highway. The owner is Bollywood producer. He has provided everything food, shelter, transport, everything.*

'पासपोर्ट कहाँ है तुम्हारा?' asked Hakimullah. *Where is your passport?*

'फज्र की नमाज़ के बाद दो अफसर मेरे कमरे में आये और मेरा पासपोर्ट, सारे सिम कार्ड और पैसे ले गए,' said Mokhtar. *After the morning prayer, two officers came to my room. They took away my passport, all the SIM cards, and cash.*

'जनाब पुने में लड़कों ने मसाला बनाना शुरू भी कर दिया होगा।' added Mokhtar with great excitement. *Sir, boys might have started preparing masala in Pune.*

'माशाल्लाह। माशाल्लाह।' said Hakimullah. *May Allah reward you with good.*

'मोख्तार माशाल्लाह।' said Morad. *May Allah reward you with good.*

'माशाल्लाह भाईजान।' said Hasan. *May Allah reward you with good.*

'अल्लाहू अख़बर। अल्लाहू अख़बर।' utters Mokhtar with great excitement. *God is the greatest.*

'अल्लाहू अख़बर। अल्लाहू अख़बर।' repeats Morad and Hasan. *God is the greatest.*

'अल्लाहू अख़बर। अल्लाहू अख़बर।' Mokhtar is the loudest among the group. He repeats. *God is the greatest.*

BOOM! A single bullet pierces Mokhtar's chest. His face stretches in shock, his eyes rolling up as he instinctively tries to clutch his wound. But it's too late—he collapses to the floor with a heavy thud. Mokhtar is dead.

Hakimullah, without a flicker of emotion, calmly tucks his Beretta M9 pistol back into the backside waist holster, his movements precise and deliberate. Morad and Hasan stand motionless, their faces unreadable, their feet firmly planted. Neither flinches nor speaks, their loyalty to Hakimullah keeping them unshaken, as the air thickens with the tension of Mokhtar's sudden death.

'ادعُوا رَبَّكُم تَضَرُّعًا وَّخُفْيَةً إِنَّه لَا يُحِبُّ المُعتَدِين,' Hakimullah recited the 55th verse from Surah Al-a'raf, in the middle of the dead silence. *Call upon your Lord in humility and privately; indeed, He does not like transgressors.*

'एक हफ्ते के लिए कोई घर नहीं जायेगा। हम पुने शहर की तबाही यहीं पर बेनालक्वामि मीडिया पर देखेंगे।' said Hakimullah. *No one is going home for one weak until all the international media shows the destruction of entire Pune city.*

'इंशाल्लाह,' Morad and Hasan responded with Jihad in their eyes. *If God wills.*

***

QD's Shisha Lounge.

Dubai.

Amidst the bubbling sound of the hookah, ISI Chief General Hamid Mir, Home Minister Iliaz Ahmed, and Maulana Fazal-Ur-Rehman, a Member of Parliament representing the hard-wing radical Islamic party, wait impatiently for a swift official apology from Hakimullah. Their faces show clear signs of frustration, having grown fed up with Hakimullah's irresponsible actions and secretive international operations. The tension in the room thickens as they exchange glances, each of them eager for a resolution to Hakimullah's defiant behavior that has complicated their already delicate political landscape.

'हमने सारी ज़िन्दगी लगा दी। अपनों का खून बहाया है। तब जाके यहाँ पहुंचे है। इतना आसान नहीं है जितना तुम समझ रहे हो,' said Maulana, looking at Hakimullah. *We have spent my entire life reaching here. One needs to shed the blood of our brothers to get to this position. It's not as easy as it looks.*

'सच तो ये है की सारी जिंदगी कश्मीर के नाम पर आपने अपनी आने वाली साथ पुश्तों का लंदन, कनाडा और दुबई जैसी जगहों पर अच्छाखासा इंतजाम कर लिया है और कुछ नहीं। और जो नौजवान अपना सबकुछ दांव पर लगाकर जिहाद के रस्ते कुछ करना चाहता है वो कब इस दुनिया से गायब हो जाता है पता नहीं चलता। ये सब होता है आपके इशारे से। ताकि आसमान में एक ही सितारा चमकता रहे. आप,' said Hakimullah. *In the name of Kashmir, you have built your personal empire in London, Canada and Dubai. You never let anyone indulge in real jihad. Because you never want anyone to take your position.*

'जितनी तुम्हारी उम्र नहीं है उससे कई ज्यादा साल से मैं जिहाद कर रहा हूँ। और कल के वाकिये से मेरा कोई लेना देना नहीं है हकीमुल्लाह,' said Maulana. *My experience in jihad is more than your total age. I don't have anything to do with yesterday's incident.*

'और इसीलिए आपने जमूरियत की पैरवी करने में अपनी ज़िन्दगी बिता दी। हाँ और इसीलिए ३७० हो गया और अब थोड़ी देर में आप आज़ाद कश्मीर की बात छेड़ेंगे यहाँ दुबई ले आलीशान होटल में।' said Hakimullah. *That is why you spent your life advocating democracy. And that is why they have removed Article 370. And now you will start talking about Azad Kashmir. Here, in this luxury hookah lounge.*

Maulana cannot argue with this hot-headed, arrogant, dangerous twenty-six-year-old kid, Hakimullah. So, he looks at General Hamid. General Hamid is in his mid-fifties, a short, underweight man with oily, gray, flat hair, sitting quietly in his dark gray, slightly oversized-breasted suit.

'ये जमूरियत ही है जिसकी वजह से तुम ज़िंदा हो। वर्ना अभी तक तुम्हारा ये सर बीक चूका होता सीआईए को।' said Ilias who was quiet for some time. *It's Jamhuriat (democracy) because of which your head is still intact on your shoulders. Otherwise, your body would have been blown into pieces by the CIA.*

'जनरल सहाब हमे इसके किसी भी काम का कोई अंदाज़ा नहीं है. ये क्या करने वाला है कहाँ करने वाला है। जमूरियत में वज़ारत-इ-खारजा की कोई औक़ात है की नहीं? क्या हमारी खारजा पालिसी इसकी इजाजत देती है? कल से मेरा एक आदमी गायब है. कोई खबर नहीं उसकी। और एक बात इसके किसी भी

ऑपरेशन में मेरा नाम नहीं आना चाहिए।' said Ilias to General Hamid. *General sahib, let me come to the point. We have no idea what he is up to? What is his next operation? Does our foreign policy allow it? Does he know about my man who has been missing since yesterday? I don't want my name to pop up in his operations. La Hol Wala Kuwatah (only Allah is powerful).*

'हम सब तुम्हे सुनने के लिए आये है। कहो जो कहना है। बिस्मिल्लाह करो।' General Hamid breaks his silence. *We all are here to listen to you, help you. Just say whatever you want to say. No problem. Just say it. Bismillah Karo.*

Maulana and Iliaz are disturbed by General Hamid's politeness towards Hakimullah.

'अल्लाह रब्बुल इज़्ज़त। पुरे कायनात की हाकिमियत, खुदमुक्तहारी सिर्फ वाहिद अल्लाह ताला के पास है। दीबाचा-ए-आईने पाकिस्तान कहता है।' said Hakimullah. *It's important for us to understand that foundation of Pakistan is its preamble. And preamble says 'Sovereignty over the entire Universe belongs to Almighty Allah alone.' Means? Means Allah hu Akbar.*

'और आपकी जमूरियत अल्लाह का निज़ाम नहीं है। ये काफिरों की साजिश है. जिसका मकसद सिर्फ और सिर्फ इस्लाम

को हमेशा हमेशा के लिए तबाह करना है।' Hakimullah continued. *And your democracy is not Allah's nizam. It's a conspiracy by infidels to wipe out Islam.*

'और तहरीक-इ-खिलाफ़ा ये अछि तरह से जनता है,' Hakimullah continued. *And Teherik-e-Khilafa knows it very well. And it will never let it happen.*

This is a direct warning to all the top authorities of Pakistan. General Hamid helplessly looks at Iliaz.

'जनरल साहब आप मेरी तरफ मत देखिये/ अगर मुल्क की सभी तंज़ीमें अपने अपने तौर तरीके से कामों को अंजाम देना चाहती है और आप इस तरह से चुप है तो फिर हमारे पास भी बोलने के लिए क्या बचता है?' said Iliaz. *General Sahab, don't look at me. If every Pakistani Tanzim (radical organization) wants to work on their own and you still choose to remain silent, then there is nothing much left to discuss.*

With a sharp breath, General Hamid finally breaks the tense atmosphere, compelled to intervene.

'देखो हकीमुल्लाह तुम्हे मौलाना साहब का साथ देना होगा. उन्हसे सलाह मशवरा करना होगा। मौलाना साहब तुम्हे पूरी मदद करेंगे। वो तुम्हे पूरी आज़ादी देंगे। जो करना है करो। मुल्क में मुल्क से बाहर कहीं भी. तुम्हे कोई कुछ नहीं कहेगा। तुम्हे सिर्फ मौलाना साहब को साथ लेकर चलना होगा। बस. वरना हम सब तुम्हारी

इस TTK के बारे में सोचने के लिए मजबूर हो जायेंगे।' suggested General Hamid to Hakimullah. *Listen Hakimullah, it is beneficial for you to join the hands with Maulana Sahab. You will have to consider him for all your activities. He will help you. He will give you all the freedom both within and outside the country. You are free to do whatever you want. You just have to join Maulana Sahab. Otherwise, we will be forced to think about your TTK.*

Maulana and Iliaz exchange subtle, satisfied glances as General Hamid's cold warning slices through the room. Delighted by the firm stand against the arrogant Hakimullah, they both sense the shift in power that now aligns with their interests. Iliaz Ahmad relaxes slightly in his chair, knowing that this intervention secures his position as Home Minister. With Hakimullah reined in, Iliaz will continue to control all operations, keeping a close eye on Hakimullah's dealings with his foreign sponsors, ensuring that no moves are made without his oversight.

Maulana Fazal-Ur-Rehman, sitting quietly with a hint of a smile, feels the burden of criticism lift from his shoulders. Hamid's stern approach means that Maulana no longer has to face the backlash for failing to control the growing influence of TTK among Pakistan's youth.

Hakimullah slowly opened his eyes and looked at General Hamid, eyeball to eyeball.

'हामिद साहब हम काम करते है खून बहाते है। 'असी गछी पाकिस्तान, बता रोस ता बतानेव सान।' ये नारा कश्मीर में हमने दिया था। अपना खून बहाया था कश्मीर में हमने। और हां, मैं सिर्फ अल्लाह से डरता हूँ।' said Hakimullah. *Hamid Sir, we work hard and we give our blood. 'We want Pakistan, with Kashmiri Hindu women and without their men' we gave this slogan to Kashmir. I only fear Allah. No one else.*

This upsets General Hamid.

'मुख़्तार की लाश बरामद हुई है।' said Hamid. *Mokhtar was found dead.*

'डबल एजेंट था वो। उसका क़त्ल होना मुआफिज़ था। सही वक़्त पर मारा है उसको।' said Hakimullah. *He was a double agent. He was destined to be killed. He was killed at the right time.*

'मारने से पेहेले तुमने किसीसे पूछा?' asked angry Maulana. *Did you ask anyone before killing?*

Maulana is ignored.

'ये बताओ बम्बई के आसपास क्या करने जा रहे हो तुम अभी?' asked Hamid. *Tell me what are you planning around Mumbai?*

'मैं ऐसे किसी भी मिशन से वाक़िब नहीं हूँ' said Hakimullah. *I am not aware of any such thing.*

Humiliation is dripping from the General's face. He grabs the whisky glass and gallops. Hakimullah is unshaken. He closes his eyes.

***

Pune – Sambhaji Nagar Highway.

India.

It's been a month, and the monsoon in Maharashtra has only grown more intense. Sheets of heavy rain relentlessly pound the windshield of a black Mercedes S-Class as it speeds along the Pune–Sambhaji Nagar highway, the wipers working furiously but barely keeping up with the torrent. The car maintains a steady pace, its powerful engine undeterred by the rain-soaked road, while visibility is reduced to a blur of water and headlights. The rhythmic thud of the rain against the glass echoes inside, creating a sense of isolation within the sleek, speeding vehicle as it cuts through the storm.

Headlight beams shimmer across the drenched highway, casting a fleeting glow on the rain-soaked asphalt, where driving visibility is dangerously minimal. Each splash of water against the windshield is more than just a reminder of the storm—it's a warning of the deep, dark, and uncertain night ahead. Yet, the driver's resolve remains unshaken, steady as the rainfall.

Behind the wheel sits an Imam in his mid-thirties, his white skull cap resting firmly on his head, a neatly groomed long white beard framing his face, and clean mustaches completing his composed appearance. His steady, meditative expression reveals no hesitation as he grips the steering wheel, eyes fixed on the road ahead. The relentless rain cannot distract him from his mission. As the old bridge looms in the distance, shadowed by the night and storm, the Imam's gaze narrows slightly, a silent recognition of the crossing he is about to make.

On the other side of the bridge, faint flashing lights pierce through the curtain of rain, slowly revealing a makeshift police checkpoint. The Imam, noticing the obstruction ahead, eases off the accelerator, bringing the black Mercedes S-Class to a slower crawl. Three police vans, parked haphazardly along the roadside, are barely visible through the downpour. Police officers in raincoats, their faces partially hidden under hoods, hold umbrellas in one hand and wave flashlights in the other, directing their beams toward the approaching vehicle.

The car comes to a halt in front of a plastic barricade, the words "Maharashtra Police" written in bold Marathi letters barely legible under the constant splash of rain. As the Mercedes slows to a stop, two officers step forward, their rain-soaked boots splashing in the puddles beneath them. With caution, they peer into the car, their eyes scanning the dimly lit interior. One officer taps on the driver's side window, signaling the Imam to lower it.

The window glass slides down with a soft, mechanical hum, and the police officer leans in, his face inches from the Imam's. Raindrops from his coat drip onto the car's door panel as his eyes meticulously scan the interior—sweeping over the clean floor, the immaculate dashboard, and finally resting on the driver's face. The officer's nostrils flare slightly as he sniffs the air inside the car, searching for anything out of place. The scent is neutral—nothing more than the faint smell of polished leather and the cool dampness of the rain-soaked night.

It's a personal car, and a meticulously maintained one at that. The officer's flashlight flickers across the smooth surfaces, revealing nothing unusual, no signs of hidden intent or haste. Meanwhile, the Imam sits unflinching, his face calm and composed, showing no trace of worry. His hands remain loosely on the steering wheel, his white skull cap undisturbed by the scrutiny.

'अस्सलामु अलैकुम। जनाब सब खैरियत तो है?' said Imam. *Peace to you, brother. Is everything fine?*

The police officer, seeing no threat and satisfied with his inspection, withdraws his head from the car window. Without exchanging a word, he turns slightly and raises his hand, signaling to the other officer manning the barricade. In response, the plastic barricade is moved aside, the rain bouncing off its surface as the path clears.

The Imam, calm and composed, shifts the car back into motion. The black Mercedes S-Class glides forward, its tires cutting through the waterlogged road as the rain continues to pour in sheets

After a steady five-kilometer drive through the relentless rain, the Imam catches a glimpse of movement in his side mirror. The reflection is blurred, distorted by the cascading water, but he can make out the unmistakable silhouette of two vehicles trailing behind him. Their shapes are unclear, but as he squints through the storm, he notices bright red lights flashing on their rooftops. His pulse quickens—police vans.

Instinctively, the Imam's hand tightens on the wheel. Without hesitation, he eases off the brake and pushes down on the accelerator, the engine roaring as the black Mercedes surges forward. The car cuts through the downpour, gathering speed, tires splashing through the waterlogged highway.

For a brief moment, the flashing lights in his mirror grow faint and distant, then vanish entirely, swallowed by the storm. The police vans, if they were truly following him, seem to have disappeared into the rain.

The ruined, dimly lit Dhaba with a large, faded signboard reading "Daawat-e-Khaas Dhaba" appears like a ghostly structure on the left side of the road. Without hesitation, the Imam turns the black Mercedes sharply into the open area in front of the Dhaba, gravel crunching under the tires as he brings the car to an abrupt stop. His breathing is heavy as he feels the seat belt tightly gripping his ribcage and pelvis. He fumbles quickly, loosening the belt with a swift pull and releasing the tension in his chest.

For a moment, the Imam remains still, his hands resting on the steering wheel, eyes scanning the rain-soaked surroundings. The space feels eerily empty, dominated by the drumming of the downpour on the car roof and the weather-beaten structure of the Dhaba. The windows are dark, and there's no sign of movement—just the sound of rain relentlessly pouring down.

Morad, crouched in the shadows of the ruined Dhaba, peers out cautiously, his eyes locking onto the approaching Mercedes. Sensing the urgency, the Imam wastes no time. He quickly jerks the wheel, guiding the car into the Dhaba's tin shade with a sharp thud, the metal rattling loudly as the vehicle comes to a stop. In one swift motion, he shuts off the engine and the lights, plunging the area into darkness, save for the dim glow of the Dhaba's barely functioning bulb.

A tense silence follows, broken only by the Imam's controlled breathing and the relentless drumming of the rain. Suddenly, the piercing sound of a police siren slices through the downpour, growing louder, closer. The Imam remains motionless, his eyes trained on Morad, who gestures for him to stay hidden.

With the siren now at its peak, two high-speed police vans, their lights flashing through the rain, rush past the Dhaba on the highway. The vehicles move back-to-back, their urgency evident, but they don't stop. They speed past, oblivious to the hidden car tucked away under the shade.

As the sirens fade into the distance, the tension lifts slightly, though the air remains thick with the weight of the near escape. The Imam, still in the driver's seat, watches and waits, knowing they have evaded danger—for now.

Morad, now joined by Hasan, steps cautiously outside the main door of the Dhaba. Both men have AK-56 assault rifles slung across their shoulders, the weapons hanging with a casual but ready posture. Morad holds an umbrella over their heads, the rain drumming against its surface, while Hasan grips a torch, its beam cutting through the dark, rain-soaked night.

Unshaken by the tension in the air, the Imam steps out of the Mercedes, his movements calm and deliberate. He opens a luxurious Turkish umbrella, shielding himself from the downpour as the rain hammers down around him. He shuts the car door behind him, the click of the latch barely audible beneath the rain. In his right hand, prayer beads rotate slowly between his fingers, a subtle gesture of focus and control.

Across from him, Morad and Hasan approach, their pace steady but charged with suspicion.

'तारीफ़?' Morad probes. *Who you are?*

'ज़ाकिर भाई ने सलाम भेजा है,' said Imam. *Zakir Bhai has sent me?*

'ज़ाकिर भाई किधर है?' said Hasan. *Where is Zakir Bhai?*

'बड़ी माज़रत से कहता हूँ की ऐसे उनका नाम लेना ठीक नही। सिर्फ भाई कहोगे तब भी तो हम समझ जायेंगे।' said Imam. *I am telling you respect. You should not take his name. You should say just Bhai.*

Hasan gets it.

'हां भाई। भाई कहाँ है?' said Hasan. *Yes. Where is Bhai.*

'भाई का फ़ोन आया होगा ना आपको?' said Imam. *You must have got the call from Bhai?*

Morad and Hasan exchange a glance

'मग़रिब के बाद से ही सारी फ़ोन लाइन कट हो गयी हमारी।' said Hasan. *Since evening, all the phone lines are cut.*

'भाई का फ्लाइट कैंसिल हो गया है। बॉम्बे एयरपोर्ट पे सब पानी भर गया है। अलहम्दुल्ला वो शारजाह में ही रुक गए है।' said Imam. *Bhai's flight got cancelled due water logging on Mumbai airport. He stayed back in Sharjah.*

This is only getting hazier in the minds of Morad and Hasan. They don't look convinced with the Imam.

'जनाब हम लोग यकीं कैसे करें?' said Hasan with respect. *Brother, how can we trust you?*

The Imam, sensing the unspoken exchange between Morad and Hasan, lets out a quiet breath. Their suspicion, their doubt, is beneath him—an insult to his stature. With a slow, deliberate motion, he shifts his gaze to both men, his eyes filled not with anger but with pity.

'सुभान अल्लाह। मैंने तुम्हारी वफादारी के किस्से सुने है भाई से। सारी तंज़ीम को बोहोत फक्र है तुम पर। सिर्फ TTK ही है जो सही माईने में पाकिस्तान को रियासत-इ-मदीना बनाएगा।' said Imam. *I have heard your stories of velour. Organization is proud of you. It is only TTK that will bring back Allah's Law.*

Morad and Hasan are still not convinced.

'मेरी निगाहों में देखो गौर से। यकीं मिल जायेगा।' said Imam. *look into my eyes carefully. Your doubts will be cleared.*

Morad and Hasan are facing a critical impasse.

'पाकिस्तान का मतलब क्या? पाकिस्तान का मतलब क्या?' asked Imam. *what is the meaning of Pakistan?*

'ला इलाह इल्ललाह।' Without wasting time, Morad and Hasan answer. *No god but Allah.*

'यकीन मांग रहे हो? देखो,' said Imam, points at the trunk. *Do you want proof? See.*

The tension thickens as Morad and Hasan grip their rifles tightly, their unease palpable. The Imam, with a calm and deliberate movement, opens the trunk, revealing two large, fully stuffed high-quality black leather bags.

As the Imam unzips one of the leather bags, the sight of tightly packed bundles of 2000-rupee Indian notes immediately grabs Morad and Hasan's attention. Their eyes widen, and the flickering doubts in their minds are momentarily replaced by the much awaited money. The Imam, ensuring that the his identity with the money, closes the bag and offers a knowing smile.

'भाई ने कहा है की केहेना मसाले में कोई कमी नहीं रही चाहिए,' said Imam. *Bhai sent this for explosive.*

Hasan still wants to do the final check.

'जनाब इत्तर कौनसा लगाते हो?' asked Hasan. *Sir, which perfume do you use?*

The Imam had been waiting for this precise moment. As he pulls out a tiny, ornate, knife-shaped attar bottle from his pocket, the velvet tassel hanging from it. adds a touch of elegance. With a ritualistic motion, he extends the bottle toward Morad and Hasan, who instinctively offer the backs of their hands.

Imam dips the crystal stick into the attar and gently rubs it on their skin. As the saffron-infused fragrance wafts through the air, both men pause, taking in the familiar scent. The Zafran attar stirs deep memories within them, transporting them back to their training days when they first met Bhai.

That initial encounter had been marked by a similar gift, a bottle of the same fragrance, forever etched in their minds.

The nostalgia of those days, combined with the heady scent of the attar, pulls them into a moment of reflection. Is this reminder of their bond with Bhai enough to quell their doubts? Or does it serve as a bittersweet reminder of the path they've walked, now standing on the edge of a fateful decision?

'जनाब, हम कारकुन है। पूछना पड़ता है। माज़रत चाहता हूँ।' siad Hasan. *Brother, we are just workers. We apologize.*

A smile is sprinkled all over Imam's face.

'कारकुन नहीं रज़ाकार हो रज़ाकार। और रज़ाकार माज़रत के नहीं इनाम के हक़दार होते है,' said Imam. *You are not workers; you both are worriers. And worriers always ask for glory. Not apology.*

The Imam picks one bag and Morad picks another bag.

'आईये,' said Hasan. *Please come.*

All three walk to the main door. Hasan is holding an umbrella for Imam.

Inside the hall, the atmosphere is oppressive. The dim light barely penetrates the lifeless space, casting long shadows on the cracked, abandoned walls. The damp floor reflects patches of light, its moisture creeping up the corners where the walls meet the ground. A complex chemical odor fills the air, sharp and acrid.

The Imam settles on the old, creaking cot, the black leather bags lying beside him like silent sentinels. Morad and Hasan stand near the cot. The Imam's fingers deftly roll his prayer beads. On the opposite wall, a map of Pune dominates the space. Bold Urdu letters spell out 'جنت کا راسته (Path of Heaven)', the phrase standing out starkly against the faded backdrop. The arrow on the map points directly to **Lohegaon airport**, marking it as the focal point of their plan. The Imam's eyes glance toward the map briefly, as if aligning their present moment with the destiny it promises.

In various corners of the hall, around fifteen young boys, divided into groups, are intensely focused on their tasks. The quiet buzz of soldering guns fills the room, merging with the acrid chemical smell that now feels inescapable. Their hands move with a fast, connecting tiny wires to printed circuit boards and assembling electronic timers. Small piles of gelatin sticks sit nearby, handled with a blend of caution and familiarity. A large Ganpati idol dominates one side of the room, its once peaceful, divine presence now transformed into something far more sinister. The boys stuff it with explosives

Adnan, the youngest in the group, sits hunched over his work, but the soldering gun trembles in his hands. His face is pale, his eyes shadowed with exhaustion. Sleepless nights have stolen the spark from his once bright eyes. The thought of death—so casually discussed in the room—haunts him, making his every breath feel heavier. The buzzing of the soldering gun is drowned out by the homesick ache for Peshawar, the warmth of his family, and the simple life he left behind.

Idris, one of the older boys, notices Adnan's hesitation. His face hardens with a mixture of authority and indoctrinated conviction. Idris, having been in this position before, understands the momentary weakness but sees it as something that needs to be crushed. He kneels beside Adnan, placing a firm hand on his shoulder.

'भाई जान घबराओ नहीं। कल होने वाले मंज़र को देखो। सुकून मिलेगा। पता है जब पहला वाला फटेगा ना तो वहां पुलिस आएगी। एम्बुलेंस आएगी लाशों को उठाने के लिए और ज्यादा अफरात जमा होंगे। फ़ौज भी आएगी और मीडिया भी। और तब ये अपना वाला फटेगा। इंशाल्लाह । सोचो क्या मंज़र होगा? हर तरफ लाशें ही लाशें। काफिरों की लाशें।' said Idris. *Brother, when the first bomb blows off, there will be police, army, and media personnel. More people will gather to pick up dead and injured. Then this will blow off. Inshallah. Just imagine the scene. Everywhere, only dead and injured people. All infidels.*

Idris smiles. But Adnan is too scared and confused to react. He tries to control his shivering hand.

'सब इधर आ जाओ,' shouts Hasan. *All come here.*

Boys quickly get up and gather in front of Imam.

'सब बैठ जाओ,' said Morad. *Sit down.*

All the boys sit in front of the Imam. Some squatted and some crossed legs. The Imam takes his time before the address.

'जो इंसांन खुद के लिए वो किसी जानवर से कम नहीं है. मेरे ये शेर, मेरे ये मुजाहिद अपनी आने वाली नस्ल के लिए जी रहे है,' said Imam. *A man who lives for himself is no lesser than an animal. But you all are my warriors. You are living and dying for our future generations.*

'वो मुजाहिद ही है जो गज़वा-इ-हिन्द की असली जंग लड़ रहे है,' Imam continued. *It is only Mujahids who are really fighting for the Ghazwa – E – Hind.*

'सेह-सित्ता की जो छह मशहूर किताबें है उनके अंदर भी इसका ज़िक्र है। उसके अलावा भी हदीस की बड़ी किताबें है उनमे भी

इसका ज़िक्र है।' Imam continued. *This is mentioned in six famous books of Sihah – Sitta. It is also mentioned in few other books.*

'कोई मकसद नहीं था पाकिस्तान बनाने का। सिवाय इसके की सईदी रसूल अल्लाह की ये हदीस मुबारक गज़वा-इ-हिन्द की पूरी होनी थी। और उसके बाद ये लश्कर पलटेंगे। यही लश्कर है जो मशरिक के लश्कर है। और कोइ नहीं बस तुम सब हो ये लश्कर। बस तुम सब हो ये लश्कर।' Imam continued. *The only purpose of formation of Pakistan is to realize the spiritual doctrine that is Ghazwa-e-Hind. And after that this army will turn back. It is this same army which is the army of Khurasan. You are this army who will fight for Ghazwa-e-Hind.*

'यही सबसे बड़ी खुश खबर है। दुनिया में कोई कौम इतनी खुश नसीब नहीं है जितनी पाकिस्तान कौम है। जितने खुश नसीब तुम हो। अब तुम चाहकर भी इससे फरार इख्तयार नहीं कर सकते। आखरी मकसद ही गज़वा-ए-हिन्द है। बात ये है की हिंदुस्तान से हमारी जंग होनी ही होनी है. हम चलते जंग में है। हर मरका जो हम हिंदुस्तान से लड़ते है वो गज़वा-ए-हिन्द की झड़प होती है। इसे कभी भूलना मत मेरे बच्चों।' Imam continued. *There is no one in the world as lucky as we Pakistanis. We cannot change our fate even if we want to. It's a fate that has directly come from Allah himself. Our ultimate goal is Ghazwa-e-Hind. War with Hindustan is the only way. We are already in the war with Hindustan. Every fight with Hindustan is a part of Ghazwa – e – Hind.*

Imam is points at recruits.

'चाहे मुजाहिदीन का कोई भी दस्ता हो।' Imam continued. *Be it any group of Islamic fighters.*

The Imam's presence radiates authority, and as he begins to speak, his words flow with intensity fills the room.

'जो पाक साफ़ नियत से साथ हिंदुस्तान से जंग करेगा चाहे वह कोई भी मुस्लमान जमात हो, पाक फ़ौज हो, अफ़ग़ानिस्तान के दस्ते हो , और किसी भी और मुल्क के दस्ते हो। जो हमारे साथ शामिल होगा वह ही गज़वा-ए-हिन्द में शालिम है। हिन्द के बारे में एक बड़ी मशहूर हदीस है। हम आपको पढ़ के सुनाते है।' Imam continued. *A man who is from any Muslim sect, who is from any country, who belong to any organizations such as Pakistani army, Jihadi Group, Afgan Group, he will be considered as our ally in divine path of Ghazwa-e-Hind. There is a very interesting Hadith about Hind. I will read out.*

The boys, their spirits revived by the Imam's words, now stand with a newfound sense of pride and purpose. Their faces, once marked by hesitation and uncertainty, glow with a quiet intensity as they focus on the task before them. Their attention shifts to the Imam's diary.

'सुनो, जरूर तुम्हारा एक लश्कर हिंदुस्तान से जंग करेगा। और अल्लाह इन मुजाहिदीनो को फतह फरमाएगा। मुजाहिदीन इन हिन्दू बादशाहों को मगफिरत फरमाएंगे। आगे सुनो। फिर ये मुस्लमान वापीस पलटेंगे तो ईसा आलेय सलाम को शाम में पाएंगे।' Imam reads a *taqreer. Listen, one of your armies will wage war against Hindustan. And Allah will bestow victory to these Mujahideens. Mujahidin will bring these Hindu emperors tied in shackles. Allah will forgive all the sins of these Mujahidin. Listen further, then these Muslims with turn back and will find Issa in Shaam (present Syria).*

The Imam, sensing the anticipation in the air, closes the worn diary with a deliberate, almost ceremonial motion.

'मुझे मालूम है की तुम सब लोग पिछले कुछ हफ्तों से ठीक से सोये नहीं हो। मुझे मालूम है की तुम्हे तुम्हारे घर वालों की याद आ रही होगी। पर मुझे ये भी मालूम है की जन्नत का दरवाज़ा तुम्हारा इंतज़ार कर रहा है। तुम्हारे एक एक के इंतज़ार में वहां उस जन्नत में बहत्तर बहत्तर हूरों का हुजूम तुम्हारा इंतज़ार कर रहा है।' said Imam. *I know that you haven't slept for last couple of weeks. I am also aware that Hindustani Army has picked up your family members. But I also know that heaven's door is waiting for you all. The groups of seventy-two virgins are waiting for you. Seventy-two virgins for each of you.*

Imam takes a deep breath.

'इंशाल्लाह जीत हमारी होगी।' said Imam. *If God wills, Victory will be ours.*

'इंशाल्लाह,' said Morad.

'इंशाल्लाह,' said Hasan.

Morad and Hasan stand near the cot, their faces reflecting a profound sense of contentment as they soak in the divine aura that seems to radiate from the Imam.

'चलो बच्चे अब तुम जाओ। मेरा भी वक़्त हो गया। बारकल्ला अफ़िक्र,' said Imam. *Ok boys, now you go back to work. I should go now. Blessings of Allah be upon you.*

The Imam rises from the cot, his movements slow but purposeful, a figure of calm amid the charged energy of the boys.

'संभल के रहो. सिर्फ आज की रात बाकि है. कल गाड़ियां आएँगी और सबको को ले जाएगी।' said Imam. *Be careful. It's just one more night. Tomorrow vehicles will come to pick you.*

'जी जनाब,' said Hasan and Morad standing inside the door.

'जनाब। बुरा ना मानो तो आप रुक रुक जाएँ। बाहर पुलिस की गश्त भी है,' said Hasan. *Yes Sir. You can stay here. There is police patrolling going on.*

'उसकी मर्ज़ी के बिना दरख़्त का कोई पत्ता तक नहीं हिलता। शुक्राना,' said Imam. *Not a single leaf from tree falls without his permission.*

He folds the umbrella with a quick tug and slips into the driver's seat, the door closing with a solid thud. The rain continues to fall, tapping softly against the windshield as he pulls away, the tires splashing through puddles on the pitch-dark highway. The car moves steadily through the desolate stretch of road, with only the beams of the headlights cutting through the thick veil of rain and darkness. The Imam slams on the brakes, bringing the car to an abrupt halt. The Imam's hand reaches for the dashboard, where a phone is tucked away. He pulls it out, quickly dialing a number with familiar ease. But there's no response. The phone screen flashes, unresponsive, leaving him with a growing sense of unease. His pulse quickens as he presses the button again, his usually calm demeanor faltering for the first time. His eyes flick to the rearview mirror, the road behind him shrouded in darkness. Nothing but empty, rain-soaked asphalt stretches behind him—no headlights, no shadows, no one chasing him. Yet the sense of foreboding lingers. He glances nervously at the phone again, his hand trembling slightly as he presses the button harder, willing it to work. Suddenly, a deafening BOOM tears through the silence. The night sky lights up in a fiery, orange glow as a massive explosion erupts from the direction of the Dhaba compound. A colossal, mushroom-shaped fireball rises into the air, the heat and force of the blast so intense that it feels like it's shaking the very earth beneath him.

'शुक्रान बारकल्ला आफ़िक़्,' words come to Imam's mouth. Imam turns back and drives away. *Thank you.*

In the pitch-black night, with rain pouring down in relentless sheets, a Mercedes glides steadily along the Pune–Sambhaji Nagar highway.

The Mercedes slows to a stop by the roadside, where a group of police officers stands in the rain. The sound of the engine fades, and with a soft hum, the window glass rolls down. The Imam, sitting in the driver's seat, peers out, his eyes narrowing as he recognizes the figures in front of him.

Through the streaks of rain, the dim headlights reveal the familiar faces of the police officers—the same ones who were stationed at the check post earlier that night. Their uniforms are damp, but their postures remain alert. They glance at the car with a sharp, knowing gaze, as if sensing something unspoken.

'घरी ज़ा रे सगळे, कशाला थांबले पावसात?' said Sambha pulling down his Imam's skull cap. *Why are you waiting? Go home.*

Sambha is a retired senior intelligence officer.

'काय सर तुम्ही पन? किती काळजी वाटत होती तुमची,' said one of the police officers in a worrying tone. *What is this sir? We were so worried for you.*

'पाठीलेना सगळे जन्नत मधी. जा ना आता घरी,' said Sambha, in his casual tone. *All are sent to their heaven. Now go home.*

'हे अयिक,' said Sambha, touching the music player. *Listen to this.*

Sambha plays an Azad Hind Fauj song.

'वो आन-ए-हिन्द आ गए

वो शान-ए-हिन्द आ गए

फिरंगियों की कौम पर

वह केहर बनके छाएंगे

सुभाषजी सुभाषजी

वो जान-ए-हिन्द आ गए'

The police officers stand motionless in the rain, their eyes fixed on the man behind the wheel. It's always a point of astonishment for them—how someone could appear so calm, so composed, after completing a mission that could have easily cost them their life. The songs keeps playing.

'जय हिंद,' said Police officers with a proud salute. *Jai Hind.*

'जय हिंद,' said Sambha, rolling up the car window. *Jai hind.*

As the window glass rolls up, sealing off the outside world, the song playing in the background becomes clearer, its melody rising above the sound of the rain. Sambha, unfazed by the tension outside, begins to hum the tune softly at first, then quietly sings along, his voice blending with the music as if the danger and chaos of the night were nothing more than a fleeting moment.

***

Sambha House.

India.

Sambha closes the gate. The metallic clang of the gate echoes briefly through the quiet, empty street.

The few hanging light-rain pyramids on the poles, shimmering from the drizzle, cast soft reflections in the overflowing potholes scattered across the road. Sambha pauses for a moment, his eyes scanning the street. The silence of the street seems eerie under the gray sky. Satisfied with the emptiness, he quickly turns, his feet crunching on the damp gravel as he makes his way toward the house, blending into its solitude.

Sambha removes his fake beard, the edges of the lace beginning to lift as he expertly slides the artificial beard off. As he wipes the remaining glue from his face, his eyes lock onto the old rose carving on the thick wooden frame of the oval-shaped Rajasthani mirror—a mirror that holds more memories than reflections.

That mirror—his father had bought it for his mother on her birthday. Instead of cutting the cake, his mother had rushed into the bathroom, eagerly replacing her faded, cracked, plastic-framed hand mirror with the beautiful antique her husband had gifted her. She had been so happy with the carved roses on the frame, roses that seemed to bloom just like her bright, smiling face.

That birthday night, she hadn't left the bathroom until she'd finished cleaning and rearranging everything. The bath soap was placed in a plastic case beneath the mirror. Blue detergent soap sat next to the floor cleaner on the corner shelf, beside the commode. The toothbrushes rested in a steel glass. A towel hung neatly on a hook across from the mirror. She made the bathroom a fitting home for her prized mirror.

Sambha and his father sit in silence, listening to the sounds from the bathroom—his mother's clinking bangles, the roaring water, and the hiss of tiles being scrubbed. The birthday cake sits untouched on the table as they stare at it for hours, waiting for the birthday lady to emerge. Finally, his mother steped out and together, they gather to perform pooja in front of her favorite god, Lord Krishna. After the pooja she often use to say, *'Birthday pooja is a celebration of the day of our birth, a moment to seek blessings from our family's Ishta-Dev and Kula-Dev. It is the day we came into this world and began our journey according to our Rashi-Nakshatra.'* It is more than a ritual for her; it's a spiritual marking of the path their lives took, rooted in celestial faith and tradition.

Whenever his father returned from his long tours, Sambha's mother would take them both to the Krishna temple. They would stand together, hands folded, for nearly an hour, patiently waiting for the aarti to end and the warm, fragrant Desi Ghee Prasad to land in their palms. For his mother, it wasn't just the presence of God that filled her with joy—it was the presence of his father. His return from long journeys lit up her world in ways nothing else could.

But the day when the news of her husband's sudden disappearance in Iran during a business tour reached her, everything changed. She fell into a deep, impenetrable silence. Hours would pass as she sat by the window, staring at his parked Bullet, as though waiting for him to ride back home. Not a word escaped her lips. Her diet diminished, and her blood pressure surged, but she stubbornly refused to take her medicine, hiding it under the bed instead.

One night, she slipped into a long, eternal sleep and never woke up. The sudden disappearance of his father and the death of his mother left a permanent void in Sambha's life, a loss that seemed insurmountable. He drifted, carrying the weight of their absence—until he met Gauri in college.

'सम्भा काय करतोय बाथरूम मध्ये?' said Gauri, from the bedroom. *What are you doing in the bathroom?*

Sambha's thoughts drift back to the present.

'आलो,' replied Sambha. *Coming.*

Sambha throws the beard into the dustbin, tucks his pistol in pants, and walks out of the bathroom.

Sambha slides his pistol into the side table. Then he quickly sneaks under the quilt, putting his arm around Gauri. She acknowledges Sambha's move with a smile. She lifts her arm to allow Sambha to slide closer. Sambha slides closer. Gauri's floral misty scent, the petal touch of her velvet gown, warm lighting, and the tranquility of the bedroom, transformed Sambha from a deadly killing machine into a small baby acting to be asleep.

Tall, long-hair, start-shape red *bindi* on her forehead, prominent cheekbones, and broad-shouldered Gauri was a college topper and state-level volleyball player. She followed her dream to become a dentist and now runs her private clinic in the neighborhood.

Gauri feels a quiet happiness when Sambha leaves his secret world outside the house. Today, there are no tense phone calls – screaming and shouting, he is not drinking alone on the sofa, and no there are no fresh cuts or scrapes from his 'secret' jobs.

Sambha held her tight. They both fall into velvet sleep.

Gauri feels a quiet happiness when Sambha leaves his secret world outside the house. Today is special, there are no tense phone calls—no screaming or shouting. He isn't drinking alone on the sofa, and there are no fresh cuts or scrapes from his 'secret' job. Sambha holds her tightly, and together they drift into a deep, velvet sleep, wrapped in the rare peace of the moment.

***

Training Center.

India.

Metal fragments fly, scattering unpredictably with each bullet that strikes the metal targets—*clank clank clank*—just ten meters from Sambha, who is in the midst of his routine training. His movements are fluid and practiced, each shot precise as he fires, reloads, and adjusts without a miss. When his gun runs dry, Sambha quickly steps aside, breaking the enemey line of fire. His right hand ejects the empty magazine, while his left hand grabs a fresh one from his holster. In one fluid motion, he slams the magazine into place, grips the rear of the slide, and maintains his sights on the target. His torso remains upright, arms extended, core engaged in a semi-squatted stance. His feet are firmly planted, pointing straight ahead, chin aligned with his gun and the target. He pulls the trigger once again. *Clank clank clank clank clank clank.*

Years of developed muscle memory and proprioceptive reflexes have turned Sambha into an instinctive, lethal weapon. Panting and sweating under the unforgiving sun at the Pimpri shooting range, the heat only pushes him harder. His body has adapted to the intense conditions—his blood plasma volume increased, core temperature regulated, blood lactate levels reduced, and skeletal muscle force enhanced. This resilience has turned him into a machine, unaffected by the harsh environment.

Sambha lowers his gun and wipes the sweat from his forehead. His attention shifts to the metallic throb of Sarah's IWI Tavor-21, who is maneuvering through a mock village, designed to replicate a POK (Pakistan Occupied Kashmir) village. Sarah, in her mid-twenties, stands tall with sloping shoulders and a slick back ponytail, free of any stray hairs. Her neutral expression is accented by soft pink lipstick, a contrast to her solid, powerful frame. She points her assault rifle toward a window, her movements sharp and controlled.

Sarah's story is one of tragedy and survival. Her parents were both killed in a terrorist attack at a Jewish community center when she was only three. Since that day, she has been raised by her nanny, the woman who wrapped her arms around Sarah and escaped the horror of that attack. Now, Sarah is eager to complete her training and begin field operations, driven by the memories of her parents. She has become an admirable and articulate member of Team 'Bahirji,' her determination shining through every action, just like the weapon in her hands.

She walks ahead, her movements precise, touching the ground softly, heel-to-toe, heel-to-toe, as she crosses the mobile shop, kebab stall, and restaurant. Her knees are slightly bent, keeping her body steady, while her torso remains upright and controlled. Lines of perspiration trace down her face and bare arms, but she remains focused, her heart beating in perfect rhythm. Her eyes are locked, furious and intent, on one of the windows ahead.

Without hesitation, she begins shooting in semi-auto mode—each pull of the trigger releasing a single, precise bullet. The casings fly out of the ejector port, narrowly missing her chin, falling to the ground like a cascade of metal. From a distance, Sambha watches Sarah with great admiration.

***

Old Building.

Landi Kotal.

Pakistan

A fully tinted black Corolla comes to a halt in front of a three-story dilapidated building on the outskirts of Landi Kotal. Almost immediately, a guard armed with an AK-47 steps out and takes position at the front of the car, while another guard moves to cover the back. General Hamid Mir, the Chief of Inter-Services Intelligence, Pakistan, exits the vehicle with purposeful strides. His expression is stone-cold as he fastens the upper button of his suit, adjusts the peak lapels with a swift pull, and slams the door behind him. Without hesitation, he briskly makes his way toward the gate, while the guards remain vigilant, scanning their surroundings.

Hamid ascends to the third floor, his presence filling the narrow stairwell with a tense energy. As he enters the flat, his gaze locks onto Hakimullah, sharp and unforgiving, like daggers. Without a word, Hamid moves to the wooden chair, sitting down with deliberate control. His veins pulse with anger, yet he caresses his lapels, attempting to steady his emotions. He takes a deep breath, forcing himself to calm down before addressing the man in front of him. The tension in the room is palpable.

'तुम्हारा दिमाग ख़राब हो गया है। प्राइम मिनिस्टर ऑफिस को क्या जवाब दूँ?' said Hamid. *Have you gone mad? What should I say to the PMO?*

'लड़कों को मार दिया गया है. एक ही धमाके में। पता भी है कुछ?' said Hamid. *They have killed all the boys. Do you have any idea?*

Hakimullah's silence only adds fuel to the fire burning inside Hamid.

'अभी तुमको और तुम्हारे सिरफिरे ग्रुप को ब्यान कर दूंगा। तीन दिन हो गए है। वहां हिंदुस्तान सरकार से कोई शोर नहीं उठा. कोई अनाउंसमेंट नहीं आयी है। ऐसा लग रहा है मनो कुछ हुआ ही नहीं हो। जो फण्ड आने वाले थे इस ऑपरेशन के नाम पर वो तक रोक लिए गए है। एक पुराने ढाबे में शार्ट सर्किट में आग लगी जिसमे कोई जान माल का नुक्सान नहीं हुआ। ये, ये खबर छपी है हिंदुस्तानी मीडिया मे। और तुम यहाँ आराम फर्मा रहे हो। तुम्हारा भाई भी मरा है इस ऑपरेशन में।' said Hamid, points his shivering finger at Hakimullah. *Right now, I can ban you and your entire group. It's been three days now. There is no announcement, no noise from India. It seems like nothing has happened. All the funds that were about to come for this operation have frozen. 'No human loss has been reported in the late-night fire in an old roadside Dhaba caused by a short circuit.' This is what the Indian media says. They are saying that it's just a short-circuit fire. Your brother was killed in this operation.*

'मरा नहीं है वो शहीद हुआ है। शहीद।' said Hakimullah. *Hi is not dead. Martyred. He is Martyred.*

'तुम अभी बच्चे हो। जज़्बाती हो। लम्बी ज़िन्दगी पड़ी है तुम्हारे सामने। तुमसे नहीं होगा। पूरी दुनिया के सामने हमे शर्म सार होना पड रहा है। मेरे हाथ में अभी कुछ नहीं है। अपने लड़कों को लेकर तुम्हे अफ़ग़ानिस्तान शिफ्ट होना होगा।' said Hamid. *You are too young for all this. Because of you, we have to face a lot of embarrassment in front of the entire world. You have an entire life to leave comfortably. There is nothing that I can do now. You will have to shift to Afghanistan with all your boys.*

Anxiety bites the air. Guards beside Hakimullah look angry.

'इतना खौफ कैसा? खौफ तो सिर्फ अल्लाह से होना चाहिए।' said Hakimullah. *Why are you so scared? one should be scared of only Allah.*

'आओ।' said Hakimullah, getting up from the bed. *Come.*

Hamid rises and follows Hakimullah, his eyes still burning with silent fury. They both descend the steep, narrow staircase, the dim lighting casting eerie shadows on the damp, crumbling walls. The air grows heavier as they approach the door, where Aurangzeb, armed with an assault rifle and missing an eye, stands guard. He grips the wrought iron sliding latch and pulls it with a strained effort, the corroded metal groaning as the heavy door slowly creaks open with a harsh, cracking sound.

The three men step into the room, engulfed by a thick, wet stench of damp walls, mice feces, and urine. The foul atmosphere hangs like a suffocating blanket. The guard shuts the door behind them and flicks on a small switch. A dim white light flickers to life, casting an anemic glow over the center of the room.

There, bound to a wrought iron chair, sits a man—scarred, blindfolded, gagged, and completely naked. His slender, short frame, covered in stubble, trembles slightly in the cold, dark room. His hands and legs are tightly strapped, rendering him helpless. Beneath the chair, a dark, wet patch of urine pools on the floor, a stark symbol of the man's fear and humiliation.

In one corner, a broken red plastic mug hangs awkwardly on the rim of a lidless, elderly plastic drum. The two objects, scarred and worn, seem like a tragic pair—like a young son and an aging father forced to coexist. Thick, coagulated bloodstains smeared across both the mug and the drum silently narrate the horrors that have taken place in this room. Torture, brutality, and the cold indifference of men who believe their cruel acts will somehow secure them a reserved place in *Jannat*.

Hakimullah and Hamid stand silently. The air is thick with the stench of death and fear, the walls stained with the suffering of countless souls. But for these two men, hardened by years of conflict, torture, and betrayal, it is just another day in the shadows of war.

The pungent smell of urine lingers in the air as Hakimullah leads Hamid closer to the trembling man bound to the iron chair. The captive, R. Bharat, shakes his head in fear, his body wracked with pain from prolonged restraint. The tight strapping has locked his hip flexors, leaving his glutes inactive, and the pressure on his lower back has bent his spine forward, forcing his head downward toward his knees. His entire body is contorted in agony, his muscles trembling under the strain, while his spirit hangs by a fragile thread.

Hakimullah lifts Bharat's head, revealing a face worn down by exhaustion and fear. He unstraps the gag from the man's mouth, but no words escape Bharat's lips. His eyes are wide, staring blankly into the void, caught in petrified silence. He knows that escape is impossible, that any last flicker of hope has long since died. His fate is tied to the eerie cries of a crow, echoing faintly through the small window in the room. The sound transports him, if only briefly, to a memory of home—a Neem tree standing tall in front of his family's house in India. The crow's calls, distant yet familiar, offer a strange comfort amid his terror.

'तुमको कहांसे मिला ये?' asked Hamid. *From where did you get this India?*

Hakimullah chooses to preserve silence.

'इसे हमारे हवाले कर दो।' said Hamid. *Hand him over to us.*

'मेरा भाई मरा है। संभा ने मारा है मेरे भाई को। इसको भी मरना होगा। इसका गला काटके संभा को रिकॉर्डिंग भेजूंगा।उसकी रूह कांपनि चाहिए।' said Hakimullah. *They killed my brother. Sambha killed him. I will slit his throat and send the recording to Sambha. His soul should shiver.*

'इसको चुपचाप हमारे हवाले कर दो। बदले में तुम जो चाहे मांग लो। अब ये दो मुल्कों के बीच का मामला है,' said Hamid, greedily. *Hand it over to us. Ask whatever you want in return. Because now this matter is between two nations.*

Hakimullah knows better than to openly defy General Hamid, a man of power and ruthlessness. He chooses to bargain, weighing his options carefully.

'कसम खाओ की तुम इसको मार दोगे।' asked Hakimullah. *Promise that you will kill him.*

'कसम खता हूँ की मार दूंगा।' said Hamid. *I promise.*

'और अफ़ग़ानिस्तान से आने वाला मेरा कोई सामान नहीं रोकोगे?' asked Hakimullah. *And you will not stop any of my trucks coming from Afghanistan.*

'एक भी गाड़ी नहीं रुकेगी।' assured Hamid. *No one will stop your truck.*

أَللَّهَ وَٱلرَّسُولَ وَتَخُونُوٓا أَمَٰنَٰتِكُمْ يَٰٓأَيُّهَا ٱلَّذِينَ ءَامَنُوا لَا تَخُونُوا وَأَنتُمْ تَعْلَمُونَ ۝٢٧,' Hakimullah uttered Surah Al-Anfal 27. *O you who have believed, do not betray God and the Messenger, and betray your trusts while you know.*

Hamid quickly realizes the delicate nature of the situation. Making false promises to a man like Hakimullah could lead to dire consequences—not just for the operation, but for Hamid himself. As the silence stretches, Aurangzeb, standing guard with his assault rifle, shoots a furious side-gaze at Hamid.

***

Training Center. Dining Hall.

India.

Breaking news flashes across the television in the dining hall. Sarah and Sambha freeze, their eyes locked on the screen as a familiar face appears—Bharat's photo. A chill passes through them both. The room falls silent as others, sensing the tension, gather closer to the television, anxiety creeping into their movements. The news anchor appears, her voice urgent.

'एक बंद कमरे की अदालत में भारत के निवासी आर. भरत को भारत का ख़ुफ़िया एजेंट करार करते हुए पाकिस्तानी फ़ौज ने फांसी की सजा सुनाई है। पाकिस्तानी आर्मी चीफ ने इस फैसले पर हस्ताक्षर किये है। भारत की ओर से अभी तक कोई भी औपचारिक सुचना इस सन्दर्भ में नहीं जारी हुई है,' said News Anchor. *In a secret trial room, an Indian citizen R. Bharat is sentenced to death. There are no details available about this secret trial. Pakistan army chief has signed on the orders of the sentence. We are waiting for the official communication from Indian side.*

Sambha stands there, numb, unable to process the shock.

'गौरी?' said Sarah, leaving the half-eaten sandwich in the dish. *Gauri?*

'Wait,' said Sambha and began walking. Sarah remains seated.

***

Gauri's Dental Clinic.

India.

Gauri stands in complete shock, her mind struggling to comprehend the horrifying truth. Her body trembles uncontrollably, and her eyes are swollen with unshed tears as she stares at the television, unable to look away from the image of her brother, Bharat. The revelation that he was in Pakistan, involved in something so dangerous, is too much to bear.

'He was always working in Dubai?' asked Gauri in her choked voice.

'Yes,' said Sambha.

'Was he working with you?' asked Gauri.

'*No,*' said Sambha.

'You always lie,' said Sambha.

Sambha kept quiet.

'Will they torture him?' asked Gauri.

'No,' said Sambha.

'You don't go anywhere now,' said Gauri.

'Yes. I am not going. I am here. With you,' said Sambha.

They both fell into a heavy silence, the weight of the revelation sinking in like a stone.

***

Home Ministry.

Delhi. India.

Pot-bellied and slightly hunched, Patil, now in his late fifties, exudes the weariness of a man who has carried the weight of the critical national issues on his shoulders for decades. His thick, round-framed spectacles sit heavily on his nose, barely covering the deep dark circles under his eyes, a testament to years spent in sleepless vigilance. Thin patches of white hair frame his head, and in the side chest pocket of his gray cotton shirt, a trusty Pilot pen is always tucked, a tool that has signed off on countless classified documents.

Patil's thoracic curve is the physical mark of a lifetime spent hunched over critical files, pouring through endless pages of intelligence reports, policy drafts, and top-secret information in his tenure with the Home Ministry's internal security division. He was the only senior officer left in New Delhi during the 26/11 Mumbai attacks, while the rest of his team remained stuck in Pakistan.

Throughout his career, he has navigated the long tunnels of the red sandstone Home Ministry building, his hands gripping the most sensitive and classified documents. Those fully wooden, warmly lit boardrooms—filled with the subtle scent of lavender and basil—are where Patil had faced some of the most daunting and desperate decisions in the nation's history.

Today, however, Patil sits in the same halls but in a different role. No longer burdened by official obligations or the constraints of bureaucratic protocols, he attends the high-level meeting as an independent contractor. Free from the chains of government service, his presence now brings a different kind of power—an experienced, untethered advisor, whose years of service have made him a living repository of national security wisdom.

'सर मला माफ करा पन भरत एक एजेंट आहे का नुसता एक सामान्य भारतीय नागरिक यांनी आपल्याला फरक पडला पाहिजे का?' asked Patil to Munde. *Sir, with due respect, how does it matter whether Bharat is a spy or just an ordinary Indian citizen?*

Munde, a man in his late fifties, is distinguished by his ever-present tiny Chandan Tilak and the sacred *Raksha Sutra* tied around his wrist. As the chief secretary in the Home Affairs department, Munde has served the nation with diligence for decades. His stern, composed demeanor reflects years of handling sensitive matters, but beneath that, he holds a deep sense of tradition and responsibility.

For many of those years, he has worked closely with Patil, whose sharp, patriotic views on national security have always earned Munde's respect. Patil's ability to navigate the most complicated of issues with unwavering dedication made him a key figure in Munde's career. Together, they weathered some of the country's most trying times, and Munde never shied away from voicing his admiration for Patil's fierce commitment to the nation.

But times have changed. With Munde's own retirement drawing near, a different kind of pragmatism has set in. He now treads carefully, knowing that any involvement in a critical project could mean an extension of his tenure—something he desperately wants to avoid.

'आजच स्पेशल कमिटी अपॉईंट केली आहे याच्यावर . त्यान्हला लवकरात लवकर रिपोर्ट सबमिट करायचं सांगितलंय . मी स्वतः त्याच्यात लक्ष घालून आहे . थोडा वेळ तर लागनच ना. असं काय करता तुम्ही,' replied Munde. *How can you say that? Just yesterday we have formed special committee on this matter. They have been asked to submit the report as soon as possible. I am looking into it personally. We must give them some time.*

Patil's expression darkens, his disappointment evident as he absorbs Munde's response.

'मला कळतंय सर पन तुम्हाला माहित आहे की मला काय म्हणायचं आहे,' said Patil. *I have no problem with that Sir. But you know what I am saying.*

'पाटील साहेब तुम्ही समजून घ्यायचा प्रयत्न करा ना . पुढच्या महिन्यात युनाइटेड नॅशन ची बैठक आहे . तो पर्यंत कमिटीचा रिपोर्ट येईन . आनि मंग सगळ्या दुनिया समोर पाकिस्तानची असलीयत बाहेर काढू ना . कळू द्या ना सगळ्या जगाला कसा आहे पाकिस्तान,' said Munde. *Patil, try to understand my position. There is a united nation conference next month. By that time the committee will submit its report. Then we will easily expose Pakistan in front of the entire world. Let the world also know what Pakistan is doing.*

After finishing his victorious statement, Munde lifted the cup in front of him with a certain sense of finality. He filled his mouth with the semi-hot zinger tea.

After finishing his victorious statement, Munde lifts the cup and sips the semi-hot zinger tea.

'जगाला काहीही घेनं देनं नाही भारत पाकिस्तान चं . त्यांला माहित आहे कि आता भारत दहा पंधरा हजार पानांचा डोसीयर पाकिस्तानला देईल आनि परत अश्याच एखाद्या घटनेची वाट बघत बसल,' said Patil. *World does not care about India and Pakistan. They already know that we will just exchange ten thousand pages of dossiers with Pakistan and wait for another similar type of incidence.*

Gangurde, in his mid-forties, sits quietly, observing the exchange between Munde and Patil. His broad shoulders fill out the double-breasted blue suit he wears, the crisp white shirt underneath adding to his authoritative presence. His crew cut gives him a no-nonsense, disciplined appearance, befitting the chief of Research and Analysis Wing (RAW).

'सर आपल्या कडे डिटेल इन्फॉर्मेशन आहे ना कि भरत ला इरान-पाकिस्तान सीमे वरून पकडलं आहे आनि नंतर ISI च्या ताब्यात दिलं आहे मिर्जाविेह मध्ये,' said Gangurde. *We have all the evidences that he was picked up from Iran-Pakistan border and handed over to ISI at Mirjaveh. Minister also knows it very well.*

Munde gives 'I-already-know-baba' looks to Gangurde.

'हे तुम्ही म्हनताय पन इरान गप्प आहे ना गांगुर्डे साहेब. आम्ही इरानला फोर्स नाही करू शकत याच्यात. कमिटीला त्याचं काम करू द्या. रिपोर्ट येऊ द्या. मला नाही वाटत काही काळजी करायचं कारन आहे याच्यात,' said Munde. *This is what you are saying Gangurde. But Iran is in complete silence. We cannot force Iran in this matter. Let the committee do its work and submit its report. I don't think there is anything to worry.*

'सर कमिटी कडून काही नाही होणार. पाकिस्ताननि कधी सिरीयस घेतलंय आपल्या कमिटीचं?' said Patil. *Sir, nothing will happen with this committee. When has Pakistan taken this type of matter seriously?*

'सर एक काम करू शकतो आपन . कमिटीला तिचं काम करू द्या आनी पाटील साहेबाला त्यांचं काम करू द्या. कोन्हीच एका मेकाच्या मध्ये येनार नाही,' suggested Gangurde. *Sir, let us do one thing. Let committee do its work and let Patil ji do his work. I think there won't be any problem.*

'म्हनायचं काय आहे गांगुर्डे तुम्हाला? तुमच्यात प्रोसिजरला, SOPला मानतेत का नाही? कॅबिनेट, कॉन्स्टिट्यूशन काही आहे कि नाही?' said Munde. *What are you trying to say Gangurde? Do you know there are procedures and protocols? Don't we have a cabinet, constitution?*

'मला तसं नव्हतं म्हनायचं सर,' said Gangurde. *I am not saying that Sir.*

Patil and Gangurde sit in silence, their faces lined with frustration and a creeping sense of hopelessness. They have tried every tactic they know, every argument they could muster, to convince Munde, but it's clear they've hit a wall. Amid this stillness, Munde slowly straightens his spine, cutting through the tension. He looks straight ahead, his eyes calm but firm, signaling that he has made his choice. It's clear to everyone in the room that this is the end—the meeting has reached its inevitable conclusion.

'मी तुम्हाला स्पष्ट सांगतो कि जो पर्यन्त कमिटी आपला फायनल रिपोर्ट सादर करीत नाही तो पर्यंत सरकार तुम्हाला कुठलीच परमिशन देणार नाही. याच्यावर ह्या नंतर चर्चा करायची काहीच गरज नाही,' said Munde. *Let me make it clear. Government will not give any permission until the committee submits its final report. There will be no further discussion on this matter.*

Munde quickly shuts the file and ties a knot around it.

'जय हिंद,' said Munde, turning the chair, he walks out of the boardroom. *Jai Hind.*

Patil and Gangurde exchange a glance.

'जय हिंद?' asked Patil. *Jai Hind.*

'ह्या सरकारचा हा नवीन कोड आहे . मिशन अप्रूव्हलचा,' said Gangurde and smiled. *It's a new code of this new government. For the approval of mission.*

Patil, feeling a sudden wave of relief wash over him, leans back in his chair. He lets out a quiet breath, his eyes wandering to the photo of Subhash Chandra Bose hanging on the wall.

***

Sarah's House.

India.

At fifty, Nanny's caring touch is evident as she pours a creamy mixture of two scrambled eggs, finely chopped white onion, crisp green tomato, a tiny Laungi green chili, and a dash of salt, turmeric, and coriander powder, onto a thin layer of sizzling butter on a hot pan. With a gentle nudge, she spreads the mixture evenly, forming a perfect, fluffy, circular island infused with the rich flavors of chili, tomato, and onion, delicately seasoned with turmeric and coriander. Finally, she reaches for a box of Yehuda Matzos, ready to serve her creation.

When Nanny discovered a torn cellophane wrapper on the Yehuda Matzos box yesterday, she nearly tossed all the boxes into the dustbin. Not even the 'Kosher for Passover' label could win back her trust in the brand. She began to question whether the owner of the company was truly a devout Jew.

She saw it as an affront to her faith and was ready to discard all the boxes. But just then, Sarah stepped in and stopped her. Upon investigation, Sarah admitted that her late-night craving had led her to tamper with and raid the city's well-known Matzos box. With that confession, Nanny's trust in the brand was restored, and the boxes were respectfully kept by the traditional Indian Jewish family.

Nanny transfers the semi-cooked, fluffy omelet onto a steel plate, the buttery, savory aroma filling the air. Without turning it over, she lightly sprinkles freshly chopped green coriander on top, just the way Sarah prefers.

Behind Nanny, Sarah meticulously cleans the open slide rails of her Glock pistol, using a small cotton patch wrapped around a toothbrush. Tiny, sticky burnt particles dislodge from the slide rail surfaces. The dining table is scattered with a trigger assembly, an empty magazine, a cotton cloth, tissue papers, and a lubricant spray.

As Sarah works, Nanny slides the breakfast plate in front of her.

'पहिले नाश्ता कर आन मंग खेळत बस त्या बंदूक बरोबर,' said Nanny and smiled. *You first finish your breakfast and then play with your pistol.*

'Ok I am eating,' said Sarah.

Sarah quietly sets her pistol and brush aside, pulls the plate closer, and begins to eat. The omelet melts into a thick, flavorful juice in her mouth. After a few bites, she walks to the refrigerator for a water bottle. Their refrigerator, more like a monument of memories, is covered with a mix of old and new photographs—tiny, torn, straight, upside down, some in black and white, others in color—capturing moments of her and Nanny's travels together. Just then, her phone rings. She glances at the Hamsa clock atop the fridge; it's only a quarter to eight, too early for any calls. She hurriedly takes another bite, gobbling down her food as the phone keeps ringing. In a rush, Sarah runs to the bedroom and grabs the phone.

***

Bahirji Complex.

India.

The office is in one of the row houses on the outskirts of Pimpri. The finely etched company logo 'Bichua' is carved on the gate. *'Bichua'* is a loop hilt and narrow undulating sharp blade dagger. The black automatic sliding gate opens, and Sambha's black Tata Safari enters.

The office is located in one of the row houses on the outskirts of Pimpri. A finely etched company logo, 'Bichua,' is carved into the gate. The logo depicts a loop hilt and a narrow, undulating sharp-bladed dagger. As the sleek black automatic gate slides open, Sambha's black Tata Safari glides into the driveway.

A brooding Sambha strides quickly through the corridor. The white accents and warm wood tones create a bright and cheerful ambiance, a sharp contrast to the usual atmosphere of the office—especially the boardroom, where the mood is anything but light.

One by one, the gruesome images flashed on the boardroom screen—charred bodies, exposed abdominal cavities, shrunken and ruptured limbs, and unrecognizable, smoldering faces, all hauntingly dismantled. Sambha, Geeta, Sandeep, Sarah, and Patil sat around the oval-shaped meeting table, their eyes fixed on the display.

Patil, the driving force behind the successful ongoing projects at Bahirji Complex, sat restlessly, his eyes darting between the gruesome images on the screen and the photographs scattered on the table in front of him. It was Patil who had named the company after Bahirji Naik, Shivaji Maharaj's legendary Chief of Intelligence, a testament to his admiration for strategy and precision.

'मोराद कोनचा आहे याच्यात?' asked Patil. *Which one is Morad in this?*

Geeta, in her coral rayon Kurti, sat quietly, her analytical mind at work as she puts the information on the screen. Though not very tall and slightly flabby, her sharp intellect and curiosity always made her stand out. Patil had recognized her potential years ago at IIT Pune, where she was demonstrating her robotics project at the Techfest. Now, as an Intelligence Analyst at Bahirji, specializing in Gilgit Baltistan, Khyber Pakhtunkhwa, and Punjab, Geeta is a critical asset, her expertise vital to the team's efforts.

'सर DNA सॅम्पल चे रीसल्ट आल्या नंतर कळेल. *Image mapping is very difficult,'* said Geeta. *Sir, we will know after DNA mapping results.*

'शोधा शोधा मोरादला शोधा. लवकर,' said restless Patil. *Find Morad. Quickly.*

'कोन हे मोराद मास्तर?' asked Sambha to Patil. *Who Morad?*

Geeta pulls up more images on the screen, her fingers deftly navigating the controls. Sambha leans forward, observing the details. As Geeta zooms in, the once blurred faces come into sharp focus.

'हा होता धाब्यात. हा ब्लॅक कुर्ता घातलेला,' said Sambha, looking at Mokhtar's photo. *He was there.*

Geeta furthers zooms in.

'हाच मोराद अल नसरी आहे. ओपेशन लीडर होता,' said Geeta. *He is Morad Al Nasri. He was leading the operation.*

Patil is eager to confirm his death.

'गीता सगळ्या बॉडीज बघ बरं परत,' said Patil. *Geeta Check the dead bodies carefully.*

Again, charred dead bodies appear on the screen as Geeta clicks further.

'This is him. I am hundred percent sure. This is Morad's body. Look at his face. He is the same guy in the black kurta. See,' said Sambha, looking at both the photos of Murad.

'हाकिमुल्लाहचा भाऊ आहे हा. मुख्तार-बेल-मुख्तारच्या अंत्य संस्कार ला तो उपस्तित होता,' said Sarah. *He was the brother of Hakkimullah. He was present at the funeral of Mukhatar Bel Mokhtar.*

Geeta pulls out a Pakistani newspaper on the screen. It's a photo of the crowd surrounding the dead body of Mokhtar Bel Mokhtar. Morad is standing in the crowd. The headline read, 'Business rivalry took one more life in the city.'

'Can you show Jamia Naeemia Madrasa please?' asked Sarah to Geeta.

Geeta pulls up the photo of the car parked in front of Jamia Naeemia Madrasa, Pakistan. The image appears on the screen, instantly grabbing everyone's attention.

'After meeting with General Hamid, Moktar's father dropped him at the gate of Jamia Naeemia Madrasa. Mokhtar went inside. And his father left. Next photo please' said Sarah.

A photo of Mokhtar getting out of a black Audi A4 appears on the screen.

'Mokhtar was never seen again. After a week, his body was recovered from the nearby well. Our agent confirmed that Morad was behind this killing,' said Sarah.

'Why would Morad kill Mokhtar?' asked Sambha.

'Mokhtar was in Pune. He went around Sambhajinagar, Jalna, Beed, and other areas and did recruitment. He arranged all the training camps, logistics, food, accommodation, and weapons. Basically, Mokhtar had too much information. And that is why he was killed,' answered Sarah.

'But Morad killing Mokhtar and then coming to India on the suicide mission doesn't make sense. We are missing the dot here. Who is this Hakkimullah?' said Sambha.

Sandeep Kaul, in his mid-forties, tall with a solid build and piercing eyes, sits silently observing the proceedings in his half-sleeved off-white cotton shirt. A former senior officer of the Research and Analysis Wing, he once operated undercover as a

Kashmiri millionaire in South Waziristan, recruiting suicide bombers for Tehrik-e-Khilafa (TTK). Now, at Bahirji, he serves as the technical director, overseeing operations in the Pakistan and Afghanistan region, his sharp gaze never missing a detail.

'पेशावर स्कूल अटॅक नंतर. ISI नि ओमर खालिद खोरासानीला त्या अटॅकचा मास्टर माईंड घोषित केला अन थोड्य दिवसानी त्याला मारल्याची बातमी अनाउंस केली. ओमर खालिद खोरासानी नि आपलं नाव बदलून हकीमुल्लाह ठेवलं. मदरसा-तुल-मदिनाला नवीन ओपेशन बेस बनवून इथूनच सगळे ऑपेरेशन चालवतो,' said Sandeep. *After Peshawar school attack ISI declared Omar Khalid Khurasani a main accused. After a weak they announced his killing. Omar Khalid Khurasani changed his name to Hakimullah and continued his operations. He made Jamia Naeemia Madrasa his new operation base.*

'म्हनजे आपन ओमर खालिदच्या सख्या भावाला मारलं?' asked Sambha. *It means we have killed Omar Khalid's brother?*

'Actually हकीमुल्लाह. सगळ्यात महत्वाचं म्हणजे माझ्या माहितीनुसार त्याला माहित झालं आहे कि तूच हे ओपेशन केलं आहे. तूच त्याच्या भावाला मारलं आहे,' said Sandeep, with his visage of wisdom and mellifluous voice. *Technically, Hakimullah. According to my sources, he knows that you were leading this operation. You are the one who killed his brother.*

'कसं काय?' asked Sambha. *How can you say that?*

'कारन पॅटर्न बघ ना. त्यानेच भरतला इरान बॉर्डर वरून उचललं. आणि नंतर त्याला ISIच्या ताब्यात दिलं,' said Sandeep. *Because pattern is clear. He is the one who picked Bharat from Iran border. And later handed to to ISI.*

'In that case, why would he hand over Bharat to ISI? He would have killed him,' said Sambha.

'Bargaining tactics. Or he wanted to become famous internationally,' said Sandeep.

A moment of desperation bites the air. The thought of being a reason for Bharat's captivity is unbearable for Sambha.

'मंग आता दहा हजार पानाचं डोसीयर बनवायला सांगितलं कि काय सरकारनि आपल्याला?' said angry Sambha, diverting his anger into action. *So, government wants us to prepare ten thousand pages dossier?*

Nobody speaks.

'व्हय मास्तर? दिल्लीच्या मीटिंग मधी काय झालं? बोलू शकतो का त्याच्या बद्दल?' asked Sambha to Patil. *Yes*

Sir, what happened in Delhi's meeting? Is it ok to ask?

'भरत सुखरूप वापस घरी येतोय. आनि तू आनतोय त्याला. तू लवकर टीम तयार कर. आणि डिटेल प्लॅन प्रेसेंट कर. लेट्स डू इट,' said Patil, in his bureaucratic style. *Bharat is coming home safely. And you are bringing him back. Quickly form your team and present your detailed plan. Let's do it.*

With eyes full of contentment, Sambha leans forward, gazing at the metallic 'Bichua' proudly hanging on the wall.

***

Jamia Naeemia Madrasa.

Pakistan.

The news of the Indian government's request to allow Bharat to meet his family made a big headline in Pakistan. Maulana Fazal Ur Rehman has summoned General Hamid to an undisclosed Madrasa on the outskirts of Rawalpindi.

'हामिद साहब रियासते मदीना बनाने का वादा किया था ना अपने? और फिर उस काफिर को उसके घरवालों से मिलने की बात करते हो? आवाम को क्या मुँह दिखाएंगे हम?' said angry Maulana. *You have promised to establish the rule of*

Allah and now you want to let Bharat to meet his family. How should we face public?

'बस बात चल रही है,' said hamid. *Discussion going on.*

'और LOC ट्रेड भी तो शुरु कर रही है? ठीक नहीं है ये सब जो हो रहा है. कह देना अपने वज़ीर को. आपकी सरकार तभी समझेगी जब हम सड़को पर आयेंगे. आप सड़कों पर खून बहकर ही मानोगे।' warned Maulana. *And also opening the LOC trade without out consent? This is not good. Go and tell your prime minister. Your government will understand only when we will come out on the roads and shed blood.*

General Hamid quietly walks out of the meeting, his expression unreadable. Maulana's message has had a profound impact on the government, shifting the balance. In response, Pakistan officially rejects the appeal from the Indian government, canceling the visa request of Bharat's family. The decision ripples through the corridors of power, signaling a turning point in their diplomatic stance.

***

Yacht.

Marina Beach. Dubai.

The luxury white yacht sails gracefully along the pristine Dubai coastline, its sleek frame cutting through the calm blue waters. Sambha, disguised as Mohammad, is casually dressed in a crisp white shirt and faded blue jeans, standing near the yacht's polished stainless-steel railing. Beside him is his long-time friend, Sheikh Zafar Abbas, elegantly dressed in his traditional attire: a pristine white Thobe that drapes down to his ankles, a red and white checkered Keffiyeh neatly folded around his head, and an Agal—a black cord securing the Keffiyeh in place.

'You have never picked up my call. And when you call, I have to come and meet you. Why is that?' said Sheikh in Arabic.

'Why do you always talk like that to me? I am not a big guy like you. A big man. I have to work hard the entire month to make my living. And I am really thankful to you because you understand this. Please forgive me, my friend.,' said Mohammad in Arabic.

'Oh, come on, stop that nonsense.,' said Sheikh.

'No. I am serious my friend.,' said Mohammad.

'Let's get straight to the business. What are you up to here in Dubai? What you want from me?' said Sheikh.

'I am tired of this job. I want to do something big, really big. I want to enter into your big social circle. I want to make big friends and crack some big deals.

Will, you introduce me to your big international friends?' said Mohammad.

Sheikh Zafar's smile, though still polite, begins to fade slightly as his gaze shifts from the sea to Sambha, his sharp eyes narrowing in curiosity.

'What are you up to? Drug trading? Human trafficking?' asked Sheikh, curiously.

'No. No. Just want to crack a decent international IT contract. So that I can also buy one bungalow near you and live a relaxed life. I am tired of running all across London,' said Mohammad.

'Who do you want?' asked Sheikh.

'Your best friend Shahbaz Sharif,' said Mohammad.

'You are not bombing India using Shahbaz Sharif? It is just a business contract?' asked Sheikh.

'أعطني عقدًا حكوميًا واحدًا مع باكستان لمدة ثلاث سنوات. لقد انتهيت. لماذا باكستان؟ لأنه المال السهل. الربح السهل. لن يسألني أحد عن الجودة؟ عليك فقط أن تدفع الرشاوى وتحصل على أموالك. ولهذا السبب باكستان ولهذا السبب صديقك شهباز شريف,' said Mohammad. *Get me one government contract with Pakistan for three years. I am done. Why Pakistan? Because it's easy money. Easy profit. No one is going to question me about the quality? You just have to pay the bribes and get your money. That is why Pakistan and that is why your friend Shahbaz sharif.*

'هذه خطة جميلة،' said Sheikh, caressing the smooth railing of the yacht. *That's a nice plan.*

' محمد، أنت تعلم أن هذا اليخت هو يختي المفضل. في كل مرة آتي إلى هنا أقوم بتأجير هذا اليخت. انظر أليس هذا وحشا جميلا يا محمد؟,' said Sheikh. *Mohammad, you know this yacht is my favorite yacht. Every time I come here; I hire this yacht. Look, isn't it a beautiful beast Mohammad?*

'نعم بالفعل، إنه وحش رائع' said Mohammad and smiled at Sheikh. *Yes indeed, it is a wonderful beast.*

Sensing the tension and aware that he needs to divert Sheikh's probing thoughts, Sambha straightens up, gesturing toward the glittering showroom visible from the deck of their yacht.

The showroom is a spectacle of affluence, with vessels adorned in sleek finishes, polished chrome, and bespoke interiors. As they entered the showroom, the showroom's manager, a sharp-suited gentleman with a trained smile, steps forward to greet them.

'This is Phantom 80m. The best in its class. Comes in four ultra-luxury cabins. Best suitable for eight people,' said the salesman, showing them the yacht on the big screen.

'Thank you,' said Mohammad, extending his credit card.

The salesman takes the card and leaves the meeting room.

'I was just telling you, Mohammad,' said Sheikh.

'سأقبل الهدية ولو كانت ذراعا أو كراع شاة. صحيح البخاري. الكتاب 51 الحديث 3,' uttered Mohammad and smiled. *I shall accept the gift even if it were an arm or a trotter of a sheep. Sahih Al Bukhari. Book 51 Hadith 3.*

'كلو تمام,' said Sheikh with a wide smile. *Alright.*

For Sambha, the path to Shahbaz Sharif's inner circle was paved with strategic patience, late-night gatherings, and an unwavering display of camaraderie. Over the course of two months, he worked meticulously to earn the minister's trust, turning their casual meetings into a bond of brotherhood. Their regular visits to the Darwish mosque in Dubai became a ritual of shared faith. Side by side, they would perform Vazu, cleansing themselves before entering the prayer hall, their voices joining in unison as they recited the sacred verses during Namaz. Each prostration, each whispered prayer, brought them closer, cementing a relationship that transcended politics.

Shahbaz Sharif, a cabinet minister in the current government, was not a man easily swayed. His reputation as a shrewd politician with an eye for opportunity preceded him. Yet, in these private moments, Sambha—still under his assumed identity—sensed a different side to him. Shahbaz wasn't just a man of power; he was a man of indulgence, one who craved the finer things in life. And it was in these cravings that Sambha found his leverage. Shahbaz's weaknesses were subtle but telling: the finest cigars, exclusive single malts, and a particular penchant for the company of beautiful women. His current obsession, Ayeza Khan, was a prime example. Introduced as a Canadian-born Pakistani entrepreneur visiting Dubai for business, she seemed like just another pretty face in a long line of Sharif's affairs. But Ayeza Khan was not what she seemed—behind her perfectly crafted persona was Sarah.

With her wavy dark hair, hazel eyes, and the elegance of a woman accustomed to luxury, Sarah (disguised as Ayeza) slipped seamlessly into Shahbaz's world. She spoke flawless Urdu with just the right touch of an English accent, spun stories of her upbringing in Toronto, and strategically revealed snippets of her background—enough to pique his curiosity without arousing suspicion. Shahbaz was enchanted, captivated not just by her beauty but by the apparent innocence that masked her sharp intelligence.

***

Sultan Properties

Ras-al-Khaimah

Inside the executive suite of Sultan Properties in Ras Al Khaimah, stacks of crisp American dollars are meticulously arranged across the polished conference table.

'भाईजान दो सी फेसिंग विलाज है और दो टाउन हॉउस आपके नामसे बुक किये है। सारा पेमेंट कर चूका हूँ और बाकि ये रहा टेबल पर। अब शेख के सामने कमसकम मुझे शर्मिंदा ना करे। सारी बातें तो हो चुकी है। सब कुछ तय हो चूका था फिर अब क्या बचा है जनाब?' said Mohammad, angrily. *I request you please don't embarrass me in front of Sheikh. We have discussed everything. I have made the payment and the rest of the payment is in front of you. I have booked two villas and two townhouses in your name. Now what are we waiting for?*

'ما هي المشكلة يا صديقي؟' said Sheikh. *What is the problem, my friend?*

'لقد فعلت كل ما تم الاتفاق عليه بيننا نحن الثلاثة. أنت تعرفها. كل شيء حلال. الآن هو الوقت المناسب لتوقيع العقد. خلاص,' said Mohammad. *I did everything that was agreed upon among the three of us. You know it. Everything is halal. Now is the time to sign the contract. Khalaas.*

'تكلم يا صديقي,' said Sheikh to Shahbaz. *Speak my friend.*

'اسمع، أنا فقط أطلب من محمد زيادة حصتي في الربح إلى 50%. بعد كل شيء، هذا مشروع مربح للغاية. أنا لا أطلب أي وديعة تأمين هنا. لا يوجد أي التزامات في شركة محمد. إنها شركة كبيرة. يجب أن يزيد حصتي إلى 50%,' said Shahbaz. *Listen, I am just requesting Muhammad to increase my share in the profit to 50 %. After all, this is a very profitable project. I am not asking for any security deposit here. There are no liabilities in Muhammad's company. It's big company. He should increase my share to 50%.*

'لماذا؟ مجرد الجلوس هنا وشرب هذا الويسكي. لقد %50 حققت بالفعل أرباحًا من هذه المنازل الفاخرة في رأس الخيمة.

أنا من يجب عليه نشر فريقي، ونشر مواردي في باكستان، وإنجاز العمل، ثم رشوة البيروقراطية الباكستانية للحصول على مدفوعاتي،' said Mohammad. *50% for what? Just sitting here and drinking this scotch. You are already in profit with these luxury houses in Ras-al-Khaimah. It's me who have to deploy my team, deploy my resources in Pakistan, get the work done, and then bribe the Pakistani bureaucracy to get my payments.*

' أنا أعطيك احتكار هذا السوق. أعرف كم ستكسب من هذا المشروع. محمد، أنا لست أحمق. أنا أيضا رجل أعمال,' said Shahbaz. *I am giving you the monopoly in this market. I know how much will you earn from this project. Mohammad, I am not a fool. I am also a businessman.*

' من فضلك لا مزيد من القتال يا صديقي. شهباز صديقي دعنا نعطي فرصة لمحمد للعمل معك. دعونا أولا نرى كيف يعمل. وكم هو كسب؟ إنه صديقنا. من يقدم مثل هذه الهدايا قبل توقيع العقد؟ الأصدقاء فقط يظهرون هذا النوع من الإيماءات. هل تعتقد أنه يمكنك الوثوق بأي شخص للقيام بهذا النوع من العمل؟ يرجى التوقيع عليه والذهاب ورؤية الممتلكات الجديدة الخاصة بك,' said Sheikh. *Please no more fight. My friend. Shahbaz my friend let us give a chance to Muhammad to work with you. Let us first see how he works. How much does he earn? He is our friend. Who gives such gifts before getting a contract signed? Only friends show this kind of gestures. Do you think you can trust anybody for this kind of work? Please sign it and go and see your new properties.*

'الحمد لله,' said Mohammad. Thank you, God.

On Sheikh's request, Shahbaz and Mohammad shake hands. Shehbaz signed the Annual Maintenance Contract (AMC) between the Government of Pakistan and the British consulting firm Infobeam Systems and Consulting Limited.

'بسم الله,' comes out of Sheikh's mouth. *Bismillah.*

***

Somewhere near the maritime India-Pakistan Border.

Arabian Sea.

The moonlight stretches across the Arabian Sea, laying a long, shimmering carpet over the tiny whispering waves. Farid Baloch, a wrinkled, shrunken-faced man in his early forties, stands alone on his weathered *Yadkar*—the traditional Balochi boat—near the tense India-Pakistan maritime border. His hair, tinged with gray, shifts slightly in the cool night breeze, and deep crow's feet mark the corners of his watchful eyes. The swollen tumor bulging on the tendon sheath of his right wrist is a stubborn reminder of the countless fish he has gutted and the grueling hours spent in these corrosive salt waters.

On the *Yadkar*, two battered plastic boxes filled with the day's catch—Mushka and Surmai—lie secured near the stern. A rolled-up fishing net is tucked at the bow, and a small, tattered Pakistani flag flutters faintly in the night breeze. The lingering scent of *Mawaa*—tobacco packed firmly in his cheek—overpowers the fishy odor of the sea, blending with the salt-laden air. A steady, passive discharge of nicotine seeps into his bloodstream, keeping him calm and alert through this tense, dangerous, and solitary wait.

As expected, a low mechanical hum breaks the silence, growing steadily louder until a dark silhouette emerges against the moonlit horizon—a figure suspended in midair. The man, clad in a sleek flying jet suit, descends, his boots lightly touching down on the wooden planks of the *Yadkar*. The small boat rocks slightly under the added weight, but Farid doesn't flinch. With a hiss and a soft whir, the jet suit's engines wind down and the humming ceases

'سلام ءُ وش آتک کن ئے منی برات۔,' said Farid in Balochi. *Hello and welcome my brother.*

'چون ئے براث؟,' said Sambha, taking out his suit helmet. *How are you brother?*

'من وشاں۔ منت واراں برات۔,' said Farid, helping Sambha in taking out the suit. *I am fine. Thank you, brother.*

'ایشی ئا بہ جن۔ ایشی ئا بہ جن۔,' said Farid. *Throw it. Throw it.*

Sambha quickly separates the arm-mounts, micro gas turbines, and the battery assembly of the jet suit and throws it in the water. Everything sinks.

'Let's go,' said Farid, starting the engine.

The *Yadkar* sails into the Pakistani waters.

***

Muzaffarabad
Abbottabad
Torkham Border
Chakoti
Afghanistan
Rawalpindi
Lahore
Multan
Bharat
Karachi Port

Karachi Port.

Pakistan.

The sun slowly breaks free from its dark shroud, casting the Karachi port in a vivid crimson hue. The *Yadkar* bobs gently in the crosscurrent, blending into the sea of fishing boats that crowd the bustling harbor. The relentless shouts of vendors, bartering over the morning's haul, ripple through the humid air, mingling with the sound of clanging anchors and creaking wood.

Amidst the chaos, Sambha has become indistinguishable from the locals. He's transformed into a Balochi fisherman, his appearance blending seamlessly—a gray *Sindhi Topi* resting snugly on his head, paired with a loose-fitting gray kurta, ankle-high pajama, and worn-out leather *chappals*. The disguise is perfect, down to the relaxed gait of a man accustomed to long days at sea.

The salty, thick morning air clings heavily, pungent with the smell of freshly caught fish and dampened wood. Farid, having already unloaded the day's catch hours before reaching the coast, navigates with Sambha through the maze of anchored boats. The throng of sellers trading their wares and buyers haggling over prices fades behind them. The scent of fried *chole roti* wafts in the air from a distant corner of the market, but neither pauses to indulge.

Away from the cacophony, they enter a quieter zone—an alley formed between vessels propped up on logs, some stripped bare for repairs, their hulls gaping like skeletal remains.

'سلام ولکم فرید,' *greeted* an old man, digging out the sand from the propeller. *Hello Farid.*

Farid stops. Sambha stops.

'سلام علیکم برادر,' *replied Farid. Hell Baradar.*

'تو گوستگیں شپ ءَ کجا ات ئے؟ ما آپ ءِ تھا تئی ودار ءَ اتیں۔ ما تئی کشتی نہ دیستگ ات۔ ءُ اے کئے اِنت ؟' پیریں مردے ءَ گُشت.,' *said an old man. Where were you last night? We were waiting for you in the water. We did not see your boat. And who is this?*

'بؤ، من پہ کیچ ءَ کمو دور شتگ اتاں۔ آں مئیں کزن ایں,' *said Farid. Oh, I had gone a little far for the catch. He is my cousin.*

'بؤ، بلے تو چہ دریا ءَ گیشتر روگ ءَ پیسر مارا ھال دیگی آؤ؟,' *asked the old man.* آت۔ اے شر نہ اِنت فرید۔ آں کجا ایں *Oh, but you should have told us before going further in the sea. This is not good Farid. Where is he from?*

'آ چہ روبار ءَ اِنت۔ بس اتکگ کہ ادا گوادر ءَ مئے گوما لہتیں وھد گوازینگ ءَ بہ بیت.,' *said Farid. He is from Robar.*

Just came to spend some time with us here in Gwadar.

'بیا اِت ناشتہ کن اِیں,' insisted the old man. *Come let's have breakfast.*

Rejecting the offer of a bite is not customary in this part of the world. Here, sharing food is as much about trust as it is about hospitality.

'ہاں من یک گُرسیں برات یے آں,' said Sambha. *Yes, I am a hungry brother.*

Farid and Sambha squat on their haunches, knees bent, toes gripping the uneven ground. The old man, his face lined with the creases of a hard life at sea, settles down beside them. He unties the corner of a square cloth bundle. Inside, a steaming packet of *chole roti*, its aroma rich and inviting, emerges.

'ترا چے ءَ انچو دیر زرتگ؟ ما درست چہ روچ ءِ شُتگ ءَ باز پیسر واتر بوتیں,' said the old man. *What took you so long? We all returned much before the sunrise.*

'منی موٹر بند بوت۔ یامابا شر نہ اِنت۔ سرجمیں شپ ءَ ما جھد کنگ ءَ اِتیں۔ آ یک مکینک یے بلے آ ھم آئی ءِ جوڑ کنگ ءَ نہ بوتگ۔ گڈسر ءَ ھُدا ءِ فضل ءَ کار بندات بوت ءُ ما وش ءُ سلامت وتی لوگ ءَ واتر بوت اِیں۔,' said Farid. *My motor got stuck. Yamaha is not good. The whole night we kept trying. He is a mechanic but even he could not repair it. Finally, by the grace of God, it got started and we returned home safely.*

مان حبيب كي ضرور ٻڌايان ته تون سلامت آهين. هو ڏاڍو ريشان' هو '.'، said old man. *I must tell Habib that you are safe. He was very worried.*

The old man, still smiling faintly, slips his hand into the pocket of his loose, faded kurta, fingers fumbling for his mobile phone.

A figure steps silently from the shadows—a lean boy in a traditional Sindhi *topi*, oversized kurta, and loose pajama. The old man barely has a moment to register the presence before the boy's arms move, a thin glimmering wire flashing in the morning light. It coils around the man's throat, tightening with a sudden, brutal efficiency.

The old man's eyes bulge in shock, his mouth opening in a choked gasp as the wire digs into his skin, cutting off his breath. The mobile slips from his grasp, dropping soundlessly onto the ground. His hands claw desperately at his throat, but the wire only pulls tighter, the garrote biting deep. The is Sarah.

'जा तुम्ही. I will take care,' said Sarah, squeezing the old man's neck. *You go. I will take care.*

Sambha and Farid move forward. Behind them, Sarah moves with silent, deadly precision. She crouches beside the dead body, her movements quick and purposeful. She conceals the body in the shadows.

***

Infobeam Branch Office.

Karachi. Pakistan.

Within a week of securing the contract with the Pakistan government, the team from *Infobeam Systems and Consulting London* set up operations at their newly established, spacious branch office in the Karachi Trade Center. The training room buzzed with activity as government employees participated in a workshop on the Infobeam Cargo Scanning Machines System (ICSMS). At the front, leading the session, was Sarah—dressed in a flowing olive abaya, a black hijab neatly wrapped around her head, black rectangular glasses framing her face, and black loafers completing her professional look. With precise instructions and calm authority, she guided the trainees through the intricacies of the advanced system, ensuring each participant gained hands-on experience with ICSMS.

'जब तक आप अपने कंसोल के इस 'सिंक' बटन को ठीक से क्लिक नहीं करते हैं, तब तक आप अपने मॉनिटर स्क्रीन पर

लाइव थर्मल इमेज नहीं देख पाएंगे। और आप उन्हें अपने प्रधान कार्यालय के किसी अन्य रिमोट मॉनिटर पर प्रसारित नहीं कर पाएंगे।' said Trainer, to the trainees who are quietly looking at the screen. *Unless you properly click this 'Synch' button of your console, you will not be able to see live thermal image on your monitor screen. And you will not able to broadcast them to any other remote monitors of your head office.*

'जब भी कंटेनर के अंदर कुछ ऐसी चीज़ होती है जिसकी इजाजत नहीं है जैसे कि ड्रग्स या गोला-बारूद या कोई केमिकल, तो सिस्टम अपने आप आपकी स्क्रीन पर लाल बत्ती चमका देगा। ऐसे।' said Trainer, clicking the keyboard and pointing to the red flash on the screen. *Whenever there is something inside the container which is not in the list of allowed-items like drugs or ammunitions or harmful chemicals etc. then system will automatically flash red light on your screen. Like this.*

'फिर आप जल्दी से इस 'स्टॉप' बटन को दबाएं और आगे की कार्रवाई के लिए अपने पर्यवेक्षक को कॉल करें,' said Trainer, lifting the console and showing them the 'Stop' button. *Then you have to quickly press this 'Stop' button and call your supervisor for further action.*

The trainees leaned forward, their fingers hovering over the controls as they followed the instructor's guidance. One by one, each participant pressed the bright red 'Stop' button on their respective consoles. A series of soft beeps filled the room as the simulated scanning process came to a halt, the digital display screens freezing mid-operation. Murmurs of understanding rippled through the group, as they exchanged glances, evaluating the results of the exercise.

***

Interrogation Center.

Undisclosed location. Pakistan.

The room is a vast, dimly lit chamber of concrete, its high ceiling casting long, oppressive shadows that stretch across the walls. Bharat hangs by his wrists, his arms pulled taut and bound to the ceiling, forcing him to stay upright. His body, stripped bare, is a canvas of pain—raw, bleeding, and covered in deep, angry gashes.

The relentless torment has pushed his mind beyond the edge of endurance, numbing his senses. Blood oozes from the open wounds on his face, trickling down his chest and limbs, mingling with the grime, urine, and feces smeared across the cold floor beneath him. Each drop splatters softly, adding to the nauseating pool of filth at his feet. Yet, his lifeless eyes stare blankly into the darkness, no longer registering the agony that holds his broken body prisoner.

'Ok listen,' said one of the interrogators.

But Bharat doesn't react. He keeps looking down.

'यह देखो। यह वही है जो तुम एक सप्ताह से मेरे साथ कर रहे हो। अब मैं तुमसे दोबारा मिलने नहीं आ रहा हूं। लेकिन इसका मतलब यह नहीं है कि ये रुक जायेगा। कोई और ये तुम्हे मरता रहेगा। मान जा ख़त्म कर ये सब।' said the interrogator, showing his knuckles. *See this. this is what you have been doing to me for a week. Now I am not coming to meet you again. I am done with you. But this doesn't mean that this is end. There will other officer who will come and deal with you with his fresh hands. You will do what this officer will tell you to do and then you will be a free man.*

The silence of Bharat is pissing off all the interrogators.

'मुझे वह तौलिया दे दो,' said one interrogator to another. *Give me that towel.*

A thick cotton towel is wrapped tightly around Bharat's face, pressing into his already bruised skin, leaving only his nose and mouth exposed. The soldier holds it firmly, his grip unyielding, while the other man steps forward, lifting a heavy clay jar brimming with water. Without hesitation, he tilts it, pouring a steady stream over the towel.

The reaction is immediate. Bharat's body convulses violently, his muscles straining against the ropes. He gasps instinctively, but the water saturates the fabric, filling his mouth and nostrils. An agonizing, choking sensation grips his chest as his lungs scream for air. His head jerks back in a desperate attempt to escape, but there's no reprieve. The unbearable feeling of drowning overwhelms him, his mind consumed by sheer panic and pain. Guttural, choking sounds echo through the chamber as he thrashes weakly, but the hands holding him down do not relent.

They continue until his strength drains away, until his tortured body collapses into the filthy, foul-smelling mixture of his own urine and feces. Gasping, sputtering, he lies motionless, eyes half-open but unseeing, as his body succumbs to exhaustion. Only then do the soldiers step back, letting the jar clink softly against the stone floor. Bharat lies crumpled, chest heaving as he teeters on the brink of unconsciousness.

But while Bharat's world narrowed to a singular focus on survival, the outside world was shifting. Unseen beyond the dungeon walls, India's diplomatic efforts began to bear fruit.

***

Safe House

Multan, Pakistan.

In the secluded safe house on the outskirts of Multan, Sambha moves swiftly through his routine of freestyle *Kalarippayattu*. His body flows effortlessly from one powerful stance to the next, muscles coiled and precise, striking and spinning in the dimly lit room. He is hidden and alone, focused on each motion, pushing his limits in silence.

Then, the stillness is shattered by the sudden ring of his phone.

'पाकिस्तान के पास भरत के खिलाफ कोई सबूत नहीं है. इंटरनेशनल कोर्ट ऑफ जस्टिस ने उसे तुरंत सिविल जेल में शिफ्ट करने का आदेश दिया है।' informed Patil. *Pakistan has no evidence against Bharat. The International Court of Justice has ordered to immediately shift Bharat to civil jail.*

A haze of silence covers the room.

'*We must find out the location,*' instructed Patil.

'*Yes, Sir,*' answered Sambha, in a clear voice of confidence.

'मसाले खरीद लो. चार दिन में . PSO तोरखम के पीछे। चार दिन है और,' said Patil. *Get the Masala from behind PSO Torkham filling station. In coming four days.*

'*Yes, Sir,'* answered Sambha, disconneting the phone.

***

Muzaffarabad
Abbottabad
Landi Kotal
Chakoti
Afghanistan
Rawalpindi
Lahore
Multan
Bharat
Karachi Port

Slaughterhouse.

Landi Kotal. Pakistan.

Sambha, now transformed into Dastageer, carries the air of wealth and authority that matches his assumed identity. Dressed in a tailored black *kurta* that accentuates his frame, he exudes an aura of understated power. A gleaming golden watch peeks out from under his cuff, glinting under the ambient light. His ultra-luxury black shoes, polished to a mirror shine, add the final touch to his sophisticated, affluent appearance.

With his sharp gaze and confident stride, he fits the part perfectly—a seasoned Bangladeshi heroin expert and an indispensable middleman for the international drug cartel.

He sits alongside Hakimullah's trusted aide and notorious drug dealer, Aurangzeb, as well as the Director-General of the Anti-Narcotics Force Pakistan (DG-ANF), Abdel Gafoor, within the dimly lit confines of an old slaughterhouse in Landi Kotal—a rugged border town in Khyber Pakhtunkhwa province. Aurangzeb, eyes glazed and posture slumped, is visibly high on heroin, lost in a hazy euphoria. Dastageer, meanwhile, feigns the same stupor, his movements slow and lethargic, masking his sharp awareness beneath a convincing veneer of intoxication.

Dastageer's ritualistic handling of the *Garda* reveals a practiced finesse. He meticulously plucks a small lump of the grassy heroin and molds it into a compact ball. Using a matchstick, he skewers the lump delicately, forming a sort of lollipop. With a steady hand, he hovers the ball above the glowing lamp's flame. The heat licks at the greasy surface, consuming the ball in a slow, controlled blaze as Dastageer rotates it carefully, ensuring that the entire ball is evenly charred.

With the flame extinguished, he doesn't waste a second. He quickly blows out any remaining embers and, with remarkable agility, cups the warm, softened ball between his palms. He rubs vigorously, coaxing the sticky mass into a solidified shape, yet, to the untrained eye's surprise, his palms emerge unblemished. Clean. There is no sign of any residue, no lingering artificiality—a testament to the purity of the ball. Even under heat and pressure, the absence of any residue is the surest indication that this *Garda* is genuine and free from the synthetic fillers that plague the street variants.

Aurangzeb's tranquilized eyes admire the rare craft and the craftsman—Dastageer.

'जैसे कहा था। एक दम खालिस है।' said Dastageer. *As I said, It's a pure heroin.*

Dastageer shows his clean palm to Abdel Gafoor, following a long silence.

'ये एक किलो गर्दा के पैकेट दस किलो अफीम से बनता है जनाब. बोहोत मेहनत है इसमें।' said Aurangzeb. *It's only when you process ten kilos of Afim that you get one kilo of pure heroin.*

'ऐसी खालिस चीज़ के लिए हमारी ओर से डिमांड की कोइ कमी नहीं होगी जनाब। एडवांस पेमेंट पे माल उठाएंगे। आप बस जेट्टी तक पहुँचाने जिम्मेदारी उठायें।' said Dastageer. *Money will never be a problem for this type of pure product. Just take care of the transport.*

'आप फ़िक्र ना करे।' said Abdel. *You don't worry.*

Abdel Gafoor's eyes remain locked on Dastageer's clean palms, but his thoughts are already racing far beyond this small, smoke-filled room. His role in the intricate web of drug trafficking is critical—he is the bridge that connects the rugged highlands of Landi Kotal to the bustling, dangerous waters of the Indian Ocean. It is his duty to ensure that each shipment, prepared and worth a small fortune, traverses the treacherous highways without a hitch, evading the roving eyes of law enforcement and rival gangs. From the unforgiving terrain of the Khyber Pass to the congested routes leading south, Abdel's men guard the convoy like shadows, ensuring that the precious cargo reaches the covert jetties near Karachi Port.

Once there, the operation shifts. Under the cover of darkness, the drugs are unloaded and packed into small, nimble boats. These vessels, manned by seasoned captains who know the tides and patrol routes better than their own homes, push off into the endless expanse of the Indian Ocean. Each boat carries with it the promise of profit and danger, braving the unpredictable sea to reach far-flung shores—Africa, the Middle East, even Southeast Asia.

For Abdel, each successful delivery means more than just maintaining his reputation; it's a lifeline to unimaginable wealth. The hefty cut he receives for every consignment is a reward for navigating the shifting currents of risk and greed.

Dastageer gives a gentle nudge, sending the pale leather bag gliding smoothly across the floor. It rolls effortlessly on its four inline skate wheels, coming to a soft stop at Aurangzeb's feet. Leaning forward, Aurangzeb grips the handle and pulls it closer. With a quick motion, he unzips the pale, purplish-pink leather cover, and the contents unfurl like the delicate petals of a morning opium flower, revealing bundles of crisp-gray hundred-dollar bills—layered tightly, like an opium pod cocooned in its velvet husk.

The sight sends a wave of euphoria washing over him. For Aurangzeb, this is more than just money. It is the pure thrill of power, of stepping into a realm where avarice is not a vice but a currency. His eyes linger on the stacks, soaking in the reality that was once the stuff of fantasy. He marvels at men like Abdel—deeply entrenched in the power structures of Pakistan—and their influential international allies like Dastageer, masters of a world few have ever glimpsed. The deal is done, the silence in the room brimming with unspoken promises, and for Aurangzeb, it feels like the dawn of a new empire.

'शुक्रान,' said Aurangzeb to Abdel and Dastageer. *Thank you.*

'अब्देल साहब मैं आपके कहने से माल तो उठा रहा हूँ. मुझे ये पता है की ये माल मुझे दुबई में मेहफूस मिल जायेगा। इसीलिए मैंने आपका और औरंगजेबका सारा पेमेंट अभी कर दिया। सिर्फ इसीलिए की दोस्ती है. हम एक ही जमात है. तीन साल से मै यहाँ नहीं आ रहा हूँ. मैं अभी भी नहीं आता. लेकिन क्या करू मजबूर हूँ. आना पड़ा. कुछ महीनो से हमारे लन्दन के फ्रांस के सभी बड़े इन्वेस्टर हमारी तंजीम से नाराज़ है. उनका भरोसा टूट रहा है. उनका केहेना है की हमसे अच्छा तो काम लीबिया में हो रहा है. वहां कम से कम जिहाद के नाम पर जलील तो नहीं किया जा रहा,' said Dastageer. *I am taking this entire shipment and also making the payments in advance. Because*

I know that the shipment will safely reach Dubai. This is also because we are brothers. I haven't come here for the last three years. I wouldn't have come now also. But there is huge pressure on me from our partners in London and in France. They are angry with us. They losing our trust. They are that Libya is better than Pakistan. At least they are not humiliating us in the name of Jihad.

'माजरा क्या है जनाब।' asked Abdel. *What is the matter.*

'इतने मुश्किल से मोराद और हसन के खून का बदला लेने का मौका मिला था हमे. चंद डॉलर के खातिर आप ने वो भी गमा दिया। दे दिया उसे आर्मी के हवाले। और अब रोज बिरयानी खा रहा होगा वो क़ातिल. बहार बैठे अपने भाईयों को मैं क्या जवाब दूँगा? वो केहेते है की अगर पैसे की जरुरत है तो हम देंगे आपको पैसे। बोलो कितना पैसा चाहिए। लेकिन ऐसा काम करके हमको ज़लील तो ना करे आप. बोलो अब्दुल भाई. बोलो औरंगज़ेब।'

said Dastageer. *We got a chance to take revenge for the murder of Morad and Hassan with great difficulty. For a few dollars, you lost that too. You handed him over to the army. And now that murderer must be eating biryani every day. What will I answer to my brothers sitting outside? They say that if you need money, then we will give you money. Tell me how much money you want. But please do not humiliate us by doing such a thing. Speak Abdul Bhai. Speak Aurangzeb.*

'बात पैसे की नहीं भाईजान।' said Aurangzeb. *It's not about money my brother.*

'तो क्या बात दुनियाभर के तंजीमो में फेमस होने की है? तो क्या बात अपने भाइयों के क़त्ल को भूल जाने की है? उस दिन ब्लास्ट में मोराद और हसन नहीं मरे थे. हम सब मरे थे. और हम सब बार बार मर रहे है. वो जिंदा कैसे बच सकता है?' said Dastageer. *So, is it about becoming famous in the world? Or is it about forgetting our murders? Morad and Hasan did not die alone in that blast. We all died that day. And we all are dying every day. How can we keep him alive?*

'भाइयों के खून का बदला तो हम लेकर ही रहेंगे। देखना तुम. मुल्तान में ज्यादा दिनों तक बच नहीं पायेगा वो काफिर। वहीँ उसे तड़पा तड़पा कर मरेंगे।' said Aurangzeb. *We will definitely take revenge for the blood of our brothers. You will see. That infidel will not be able to survive for long in Multan. We will torture him to death there.*

'इंशाल्लाह। जरूर। जितना पैसा चाहिए मैं लाकर दूंगा। इंशाल्लाह कोई कमी नहीं होगी आपको।' said Dastageer. *Yes. I will arrange all the money that you need.*

'आप हमारे बिज़नेस का ख्याल करे. हमारे फंडिंग का ख्याल करे. देखना जल्दी ही उनको खबर मिल जाएगी।' assured Abdel. *You take care of our business. Take care of our funding. You will see that they will get the news soon.*

'इंशाल्लाह। इससे एक पैगाम पहुंचेगा दुनिया भर में. एक भरोसा आएगा। और फंडिंग आएगी। और बिज़नेस होगा।' said Dastageer. *Inshallah. This will send a message across the world. There will be trust. More funding will come. More business will happen.*

'इंशाल्लाह।' said Aurangzeb, in a stoned hazy voice. *Inshallah.*

The mention of the killing in Multan Jail sends a sudden, icy tremor down Dastageer's spine. Unbidden, his mind drags forth the vivid memories of those suffocating months spent in the infamous Multan Central Jail (MCJ) on drug trafficking charges. The stench of the rotting toilets still lingers in his nostrils, mingling with the putrid air of overcrowded, sweat-drenched dormitories crammed with every manner of criminal. He can still feel the rough texture of the walls—unrepaired, unpainted—and the cold bite of the rusted iron grills that penned them in. The sinister reality of MCJ flashes before him: a world where drugs and weapons flowed like water, where prostitution and

Bacha Bazi festered unchecked, and where the grotesquely obese, corrupt guards watched it all with indifferent, greedy eyes, sucking the life and money from those ensnared behind bars.

But outwardly, Dastageer's expression remains stone cold. His demeanor is composed, detached— as if the mention of that wretched place has no power over him. After all, he is Dastageer.

'तो फ़ीर आज रात को गाडी आएगी?' *So, the truck will come tonight? as*ked Dastageer.

'हाँ,' assured Aurangzeb. *Definitely.*

'बारकल्ला अफिक,' said Dastageer. *The blessing of Allah upon you.*

Aurangzeb wordlessly offers his tobacco pipe, the carved wooden stem glinting faintly under the dim light. Dastageer accepts it without hesitation, taking a drag.

***

Nawabpur.

Multan. Pakistan.

Sambha, now transformed into Mehfil Ali, cuts an arresting figure in his new guise. He sits cross-legged on the veranda, draped in a flowing black *Salwar Kurta*, the soft red checked scarf resting casually on his shoulders. His long, curly hair cascades down, framing his face, while a thick, gracefully curved black mustache adds a touch of authority to his appearance. The deep Kajal lining his eyes intensifies his gaze, giving him an enigmatic presence. Around his neck, a string of black beads dangles.

It's the veranda of his old friend Albert David's bungalow, a crumbling relic nestled near the sprawling garbage dumping area of Nawabpur, Multan. From a distance, no one would suspect that Mehfil Ali, with his relaxed posture and casual attire, is anything more than another drifter in this forgotten corner of Multan.

For Albert, Mehfil Ali is a rich and caring *Khanaabadosh* (Gypsy) elder brother. Mehfil is his last man standing. Albert is a strong, tall, and hard-working man. He is the owner of Multan Waste Management Company. Albert is also the president of the All-Pakistan Sweeper Association (APSA). He also fights for minority rights in Pakistan. When the Chief Minister of KPK publicly said that only non-Muslims would do a Sweeper job, it was Albert who did a massive protest. Mehfil took care of his family when Albert was in jail.

For Albert, Mehfil Ali is more than just an old friend in disguise—he is the embodiment of loyalty and kinship, a rich and caring *Khanaabadosh* elder brother who has stood by him through the fiercest storms. In the labyrinth of Albert's chaotic life, Mehfil has always been the last man standing. When others turned their backs or cowered away, Mehfil remained—a silent sentinel, watching over his family when Albert languished behind bars.

Albert, on the other hand, is a formidable presence—strong, tall, and tireless in his work. He holds a unique position of power and influence as the owner of the Multan Waste Management Company, navigating the intricate and often corrupt systems of the city's sanitation sector. But beyond his business acumen, Albert's true strength lies in his courage to confront injustice head-on. As the president of the All-Pakistan Sweeper Association (APSA), he's the voice of thousands—championing the rights of sanitation workers and fighting tirelessly for the oppressed minorities of Pakistan.

His moment of defiance against the Chief Minister of KPK cemented his role as a symbol of resistance. When the Chief Minister declared that only non-Muslims should take up sweeper jobs, it was Albert who mobilized a massive protest, shaking the very foundations of prejudice and discrimination. He stood tall, demanding respect and dignity for every worker—regardless of faith or creed. His arrest, though a personal setback, became a rallying cry for many. And in those dark months, when jail walls threatened to smother his spirit, it was Mehfil Ali who stepped in, ensuring that Albert's family never felt the sting of abandonment.

For Albert, Mehfil is more than a brother in disguise. He is a lifeline. A protector. A man whose presence alone is a reassurance that, no matter how treacherous the path, he will never walk it alone.

'इतना बड़ा जेल है. बोहोत सारे मजदुर लगते होंगे?' said Mehfil, sipping hot tea from saucer. *It's such a big prison and how do you manage alone.*

'भाईजान जेल के पीछे की तरफ जो मेन सीवर लाइन्स है वो साफ़ रही तो सब ठीक रेहेता है. बाकि बाथरूम टॉयलेट में रोज पानी मारा की साफ़ हो जाता है। उसके लिए मेरे लगभग दस आदमी काफी हो जाते है। और फिर हमलोग ये नहीं करेंगे तो और कौन करेगा? ये काम सिर्फ क्रिस्चन लोगो का है।, said Albert.

'कर तो तुम बोहोत कुछ सकते हो. मुझे एक दिन के लिए तुम्हारे साथ जेल के अंदर ले चलो। बोहोत साल पुराना हिसाब चुकता करना है।' said Mehfil.

'क्या करना है भाईजान?' asked Albert. *What do you want me to do?*

'कुछ नहीं। सिर्फ मुझे तुम्हारे साथ अंदर ले चलो।' said Mehfil. *Nothing, just take me with you.*

'अंदर कोई खून खराबा तो नहीं होगा ना? मुझे मुश्किल में मत डालो भाई,' said Albert. *Will there be any fight? Please don't put me in trouble brother.*

'तुम्हारे लोगो का ना तो ग्रुप इन्शुरन्स है. ना तो सोशल सिक्योरिटी कवर है. और ना तो EOBI कार्ड है। फिर भी टेंशन ले रहे हो बिरादर। मैं हूँ ना,' said Mehfil. *You people don't have group insurance, neither have social security benefits, nor EOBI card. And still, you are worried.*

Mehfil takes out a large bundle of American dollars and gives it to Albert. He quickly takes the bundle and tugs it into his pocket.

'कितना काम करोगे तुम। साडी जिंदगी जेलों की गन्दगी साफ करने में लगा दी. तुमको अपने परिवार के साथ कुछ समय बिताना चाहिए। तुम उन्हें खरीदारी के लिए ले जाएं। आखिरकार, वो भी तो दूसरों की तरह जीना चाहते होंगे। ये घर देखो। ठीक करो इसको। भाई हूँ तुम्हारा। भाभी और बच्चों के खातिर कुछ भी कर सकता हूँ. और पैसे चाहिए तो और दूंगा। ये महफ़िल भाई खाना बदहोश है गरीब नहीं।' said Mehfil. *You have spent your whole life cleaning the filth of these jails. Now you should spend some time with your family. You must take them for shopping. You must renovate this bungalow. After all, they too would want to live like others. I am your brother. If you need more money for Bhabhi and the children, I will give you more. This Mehfil Bhai Khana is a drunkard, not a poor person.*

'मगर भाईजान अंदर काम क्या है,' asked Albert. *What are you up to my brother?*

'देखो अल्बर्ट अगर जेलर तुम्हारे सफाई ठेके को कैंसिल भी कर देता है तब भी तुम बिना कोई काम किए इस पैसे पर दो साल आरामसे अपना घर चला सकते हो। फिर करते रहना तुम्हारी माइनॉरिटीज की हक़ की लड़ाई। कुछ नहीं होगा।' said Mehfil. *Look, Albert, even if the jailor cancels your cleaning contract, you can easily run your house for two years on this money without doing any work. Then you can keep fighting for the rights of your community. Nothing will happen.*

'मै बस इतना जानता हूँ की आज मैं अगर जिन्दा हूँ तो आपकी वजह से हूँ. बाकि ये जान हाजिर है आपके लिए भाईजान। कब जाना है?' said Albert. *I just know that if I am alive today, it is because of you. The rest is up to you brother. When you want to come?*

***

Multan Central Jail.

Pakistan.

It's just past six in the morning, and the Multan Central Jail is already in turmoil. Shouts and curses echo through the corridors as the foul stench of overflowing toilets hangs heavy in the air. Something has gone terribly wrong with the main drainage line. Inmates and guards scramble in agitation, but there's little they can do. The situation demands urgent intervention, and soon, the Multan Waste Management Company workers are summoned.

Albert and his team arrive at the main gate, their green MWMC t-shirts and blue track pants marking them as the unsung custodians of order amid the chaos. The guards, familiar with their routine, perform a quick yet thorough inspection of their IDs and tools before waving them through. Mehfil Ali, blending seamlessly into the crew, keeps his gaze low, the blue cap pulled just enough to shadow his face. Today, he's no elder brother, no gypsy wanderer—just another worker in the sanitation brigade, stepping into the bowels of a place he knows too well.

They pass through the heavy iron gates, stepping into the suffocating confines of the jail, armed with little more than shovels, wrenches, and their resolve. The morning has just begun, and they have a mountain of filth to tackle, but none show hesitation. For Albert, Mehfil, and the rest of the team, it's just another day in a world where decay never sleeps.

Trusting his instincts, Mehfil directs his attention toward the western dormitory.

'जनाब मैं उधर जाता हूँ ,' said Mehfil. *Sir, can I go there?*

Albert gives a subtle nod. Mehfil wastes no time, grabbing a mop and bucket before heading briskly toward the dormitory. Peering through the iron grill, his eyes scans. The cramped space is packed with bodies—some curled under thin sheets, others wrapped in flimsy plastic to ward off the cold. Shapes and shadows blend together, making it almost impossible to distinguish faces in the densely packed dormitory. His eyes sweep the room cautiously, searching for any sign, any clue, hidden amidst the restless slumber of the prisoners.

A police officer taps Mehfil from behind.

'यहाँ खड़े खड़े क्या कर रहे हो?' said Police officer. *What are you looking?*

'जनाब उलटी की बू आ रही है . वही देख रहा हूँ' said Mehfil. *Sir, its smelling like vomit. I am checking.*

'वो गटर देखो पहले।' said the Police. *Go and check the gutter first.*

Mehfil immediately walks to the gutter.

Mehfil crouches low, straddling the narrow drain channels outside the toilets near the dormitory. He reaches into the murky water, plucking out floating matchsticks, cigarette butts, and stained *gutkha* wrappers—his actions a mere guise for the watchful eyes around him. As he works, his gaze flickers constantly, observing every movement, every twitch of the prisoners nearby. But so far, there's been nothing unusual.

Minutes stretch into a long, tense wait. Then, at last, a creaking sound breaks the stillness as one of the bathroom doors swings open. Mehfil glances up, eyes narrowing as a figure emerges. A bald, pale-skinned man stumbles out, his swollen toes dragging sluggishly across the floor. His sunken eyes, hollow and lifeless, look at nothing in particular. His back is hunched. He is Bharat.

'ये देखो. देखो तुस्सी. ना कुछ कपड़े है. ना कुछ मेडिकल है. मैं हाल में हूं पाजी। मजबूरी है करना. करना पैंदा है. साड्डी कोई कदर नहीं करते। सारे सानू समझते है नीचे। निच. कोई बंदा साड्डा नाल सालुक चंगा नहीं करदा। आया नई, यारा दास रुपय लेलो, लस्सी पीलो, चाह पीलो। देखो तुस्सी. (ये देखो। ये देखो। हमारे पास ढंग के कपड़े नहीं हैं। न ही हमारे पास कोई मेडिकल सुविधा है। ये हमारी हालत है, मेरे दोस्त। फिर भी हमें ये काम करना पड़ता है। कोई हमारी परवाह नहीं करता। सबको लगता है कि हम हम अछूत हैं। कोई भी हमारे साथ सम्मान से पेश नहीं

आता। कोई नहीं कहता कि ये दस रुपये लो और चाय पियो या छाछ पियो। सुन रहे हो?' said Mehfil, loudly enough to reach Bharat. *Look at this Sir. We don't have good clothes. Nor is there any government medical facility for us. I am in a difficult state. I am forced to do this work. This is terrible. No one cares about us. We are untouchables. No one comes to us and says 'Come my friend take this money, drink some lassi, drink tea.*

But Bharat remains unfazed, oblivious to Mehfil's presence. His eyes, dull and unseeing, refuse to meet the gaze that silently reaches out to him. Bharat simply limps forward, heading back to the dormitory as if tethered to an invisible chain.

Mehfil doesn't let the opportunity slip away. With a calculated move, he lifts the heap of accumulated garbage and casually follows, letting a few pieces spill deliberately onto the ground near Bharat's path. Kneeling near Bharat, he begins to pick up the fallen debris.

'थांब भरत. वर नको भघु. ख्वाजा फरीद मध्ये भेट. वीर बाल दिवसाला. हाताला झटका देऊन सांग।' said Mehfil, quickly and clearly. *Stop Bharat. Do not look up. Meet in Khawaja Fareed on Veer Bal Diwas. Shake your hand to confirm.*

Bharat's shake his hand.

'छत्रपति शिवाजी महाराज कि जय,' said Mehfil and walked away with the garbage. *Chatrapati Shivaji Maharaj Ki Jai.*

Bharat limps in the direction of the dormitory.

'छत्रपति शिवाजी महाराज कि जय,' *Chatrapati Shivaji Maharaj Ki Jai.* whispers Bharat in his broken voice. Bharat's voice did not reach Sambha. But Sambha's voice has lifted Bharat's spirit. Khawaja Fareed Hospital got registered in his mind.

The post-lunch hours are reserved for rest, even for the most hardened inmates, and for Akhtar Baloch, it's no different. Stretched out luxuriously on a plush carpet, the notorious prisoner enjoys a level of comfort unimaginable for most. Serving a life sentence means little when you're backed by a powerful family and have deep ties with influential local politicians. His dangerous reputation and connections have bought him privileges, turning his cell into a private kingdom. The guards steer clear; the other inmates avert their eyes. He is the undisputed boss of the dormitory, a man whose wrath is felt long after the bruises fade. No one speaks to Akhtar unless spoken to—he's a bone-breaker, a man whose punishments leave scars, both physical and mental.

Beside him, hunched and wary, sits Bharat, the only one who dares to linger in Akhtar's shadow.

The air between them is heavy with unspoken history—old friends who've traveled far down dark paths. Bharat's eyes flit to Akhtar's outstretched arm. Gingerly, he reaches over and lifts the bulky, expensive wristwatch from Akhtar's wrist, checking the time.

'ये डिजिटल घडी है हिंदी बरादर। मेरे भाई ने दुबई से लायी है। मैंने जब दो फौजी मुखबिरों को मारा था तब उसने गिफ्ट की थी ये घडी।' said Akhtar Baloch, relaxing on the carpet. *It's a digital watch my Hindi brother. My brother brought me from Dubai. He gifted me when I killed two army informers.*

'बोहोत अछि है मेरे भाई,' said Bharat. *It's a very nice watch my brother.*

Bharat needed to know the exact date and time to begin counting the days. The only thing he could rely on for that was Akhtar's watch.

***

Jaan Faluda.

Qissa Khawani Bazaar. Peshawar.

Jaan Restaurant is renowned for its Kulfi Faluda, drawing people from all over to indulge in the creamy delight. Amidst the bustling crowd, Sambha sits quietly, transformed into Nadir Ali, a nondescript small-time property broker. His red-blue checked shirt and black jeans blend in effortlessly, while his hair, neatly parted in the middle, frames his face. A cheek bulging with gutkha completes his disguise, masking the sharp eyes that miss nothing.

Across from him sits Rauf Klasra, a *karkun* in the Town Planning Department of Peshawar.

اک کاغذ وی جے کسے سرکاری دفتر نال تعلق رکھدا اے تے بڑا اہم تے بڑا خفیہ ہو جاندا اے۔ تے تسی سرکاری ہسپتال دا پورا ترتیب تے بلیو پرنٹ منگ رئے او. کی تہانوں کوئی اندازہ اے کہ ایہ میرے لی کِنا خطرناک اے؟ ریکارڈ روماں ول بہت ساریاں اکھاں گھور رئی اے۔ دستاویز کڈھن دے ہر مرحلے تے مینوں پچھیا جائے گا؛ مقصد کی اے؟ ایہہ کاغذ تہانوں کیوں چاہیدا اے؟ جنہاں لوکاں نوں میں ایہہ دستاویزات سونپ رہیا واں اوہناں دی شناخت. ہر شے غیر قانونی اے۔ اس لین دین چ کوئی وی چیز قانونی نئیں اے۔ تسی کجھ وی منگدے او پر کوئی ترتیب یا کوئی بلیو پرنٹ نئیں۔ نئیں۔ ایہ سوال توں باہر اے ,' said Rauf in Peshawari Punjabi. *Even a single paper becomes very important and very secret if it belongs to any government office. And you are asking for the entire layout and blueprint of the government hospital. Do you have any idea how much risky it is for me? There are so many eyes staring at the record rooms. At every step of taking out the document I will be quested; What is the purpose? Why do you want these papers? Identity of the people to whom I am handing over these documents. Everything is illegal. Nothing is legal in this transaction. You ask for anything but not any layout or any blueprint. No. It's out of the question.*

ویسے وی ایہہ اک بہت پرانا ہسپتال اے۔ رؤف صاحب لے آؤٹ تے بلیو پرنٹ ساڈی کمپنی دا اینا اہم نئیں اے۔ رؤف صاحب ایہہ ہمیشہ چنگا ہوندا اے کہ تُسی اپنا ڈیزائن کرنا شروع کرن توں پہلاں مختلف رلدے ملدے ڈھانچیاں دا مطالعہ کرو۔ میرے کول دوجے وڈے ہسپتالاں دے بلیو پرنٹ پہلے ای موجود ہن۔ میری کمپنی نوں ہور ترتیب دی لوڑ نئیں اے۔ ایہہ صرف اینا اے کہ جے میں کمپنی نوں ہور ترتیب جمع کراواں گا تے مینوں ہور بروکریج ملے گی۔ میں ترتیب پچھ رہیا واں تاکہ مینوں ہور پیسے مل سکن۔ جے مینوں ہور پیسے ملن گے تے فیر رؤف صاحب نوں ہور پیسے ملن گے۔ دن دے اخیر تے ایہہ بہت پرانا سرکاری ہسپتال اے۔ کمپنی نوں اپنے ترتیب دی کیوں لوڑ ہووے گی۔ ایہہ میں آں جھڑا اوہناں نوں پیسے لئی ترتیب ویچ رہیا واں۔ چلو پیسہ کما لیندے آں۔ رؤف صاحب۔ ایہہ گل اے *said Nadir, in Peshawari Punjabi. Anyways it's a very old hospital. Rauf Sahab layout and blueprint is not that important of our company. Rauf Sahab it's always better to study the different similar structures before you start designing your own. I already have the blueprints of the other big hospitals with me. My company don't need any more layouts. It is just that if I submit more layouts to the company, I will get more brokerage. I am asking the layout so that I can get more money. If I get more money than Rauf Sahab will get more money. At the end of the day, it very old government hospital. Why company would need its layout. It is me who is selling them the layout for money. Let us make money. Rauf Sahab. This is the point.*

'دستاویزات کروان لئی دوجے عہدیداراں نوں کنا پیسہ دتا اے,' said Rauf. *How much have paid to other officials to get the documents.*

'ریٹ اک ہزار ڈالر فی ترتیب اے۔ اوہ وی نقد رقم چ۔ پنج سو ڈالر تیرے ہون گے۔ اسی کرئیے رؤف صاحب۔ نادر نے آکھیا,' said Nadir. *It is french company. The rate is one thousand dollars per layout. That too in cash. Five hundred dollars will be yours. Let us do it Rauf Sahab.*

'انشاءاللہ,' said Rauf. *Inshallah.*

'اک ہور فلودہ,' shouts Rauf, to the waiter. *One more falooda.*

Sarah, dressed in a vibrant turquoise *salwar kameez* paired with a light blue scarf draped loosely over her head, blends effortlessly into the Flooda lovers around them.

***

Safe House.

Multan. Pakistan.

A layout of Khawaja Fareed Hospital is displayed on Sambha's laptop screen. Sarah and Patil are connected remotely.

'ऑपरेशन थिएटरच्या अगोदर ही छोटी रूम आहे. ही आपल्यासाठी महत्वाची ठरू शकते. ओपरेशन थियटरला सेपरेट दरवाजे आहेत. हा डॉक्टर साठी आहे. हा इतर स्टाफ साठी आहे. आणि हा पेशंट साठी,' said Sarah. *There is this large size ante room right before the operation theater. It can be useful. OT is having separate entrances. This one is for surgeons, this one is for other staff, and this is where patients enter on the stretcher.*

'अजून एक रेकी ची गरज आहे का?' asked Patil. *You need one more recce?*

'I am ready Sir,' said Sambha.

'तो जर नाही पोहोचला तर काय करनार आपन? प्लॅन बी काय आहे आपला?' asked Patil. *What are we going to do if Bharat doesn't reach here? What is our next action plan?)'*

That thought never occurred to Sambha.

'Sir, I know him very well,' said Sambha.

'About plan B, I will let you know Sir,' said Sambha after a long silence.

***

Schools.

India

It's around seven in the morning, and across India, school stages are set for one of the most revered children's performances of the year. Clad in traditional Sikh attire, young boys and girls stand proud, embodying the spirit of valor and resilience. Today, they honor the martyrdom of Sahibzada Zorawar Singh and Sahibzada Fateh Singh, the younger sons of Guru Gobind Singh Ji.

The story being told is one of unwavering courage. On this day, December 25th, 1705, the two young brothers, along with their grandmother, Mata Gujari Ji, were captured by the Mughals under the command of Aurangzeb. When they refused to abandon their faith and convert to Islam, they were sentenced to death. The boys were mercilessly bricked alive within a narrow enclosure, choosing martyrdom over surrender. Zorawar Singh was only nine years old, and Fateh Singh, a mere six.

The sacrifice of these two young souls, steadfast in the face of tyranny, is commemorated as an act of ultimate bravery and devotion to *Dharma*. For these little lions performing on stage, their voices strong and their postures firm, it is more than just a play. It is a tribute to the courage of two children who stood tall against oppression, inspiring generations to come.

This is the day Bharat must meet Sambha.

***

Multan Central Jail.

Pakistan.

The morning chaos unfolds as inmates go about their routine—smoking *beedis*, rolling up carpets, wiping away last night's vomit, and bickering over borrowed mugs while jostling for their turn at the overflowing toilets. A couple of mentally unstable prisoners stand silently by the iron grills, gazing vacantly at the world outside. Amidst the noise and disorder, Bharat sits quietly with Akhtar in a dimly lit corner, a stillness between them that contrasts sharply with the turmoil around.

'भाई मानो मेरी बात. तुम्हारा एहसान रहेगा मुझपर। कुछ मत सोचो।' said Bharat. *Brother, I beg you. Please do as I said. Don't think much.*

'ऐ क्या करवा रहे हो भाई?,' said Akhtar. *Brother, I cannot do this.*

'तुम्हे तुम्हारे खुदा वास्ता,' said Bharat. *For God's sake, do it.*

Bharat's request has placed Akhtar in a deep moral quandary. His jaw tightens as he contemplates the weight of the decision. What Bharat has asked of him doesn't sit right—it grates against his principles, his sense of honor. But as a proud Baloch, refusing a friend, especially one like Bharat, isn't an option.

His loyalty outweighs his reluctance. With a grim resolve, Akhtar wraps his thick fingers around the cold, heavy iron rod. His face contorts with anger—not at Bharat, but at the position he's been put in. The words spill out of his mouth, loud and venomous, as he begins hurling abuses at Bharat, his voice echoing across the dormitory.

'साले चोर. मेरी घडी चुराता है। तुझे दिखता हूं। रुख।' said Akhtar. *You bloody thief. Wait I will show you.*

Akhtar turns to other inmates.

'सब सुनो। इस कुत्ते ने मेरी घडी चुराने की कोशिश की। अब देखो क्या होता है इसका।' screamed Akhtar. *You all listen. This dog has tried to steal my watch. Now you see what I am going to do with him.*

Prisoners gather around Akhtar. No one says anything. All are anticipating an entertaining moment in their stagnant lives. Bharat remains silent.

'टांग पकड़ो इसकी। कसके पकड़ो।' said Akhtar to one of the inmates. *Hold his leg. Tightly hold his leg.*

On of the man quickly holds Bharat's left ankle and pulls it outward.

'मेरे सामान को कभी भी हाथ नहीं लगाना। कभी नहीं,' said angry Akhtar. *Never try to come near this corner again. Never.*

Bharat is silent.

Akhtar's grip tightens around the iron rod as his face twists into a mask of forced rage. With a roar, he lifts the rod high and brings it crashing down on Bharat's leg. The sound of metal meeting flesh and bone reverberates through the dormitory. Bharat clenches his teeth, his body tensing with each brutal strike. Akhtar doesn't relent; blow after blow lands on the same spot, sending shockwaves of pain coursing through Bharat's frame.

Then, with a sickening crunch, Bharat's fibula gives way. He cries out in agony, a guttural sound that cuts through the tense silence of the watching prisoners. His leg throbs violently, the bone shattered beneath the relentless assault.

'लेके जाओ इसको। बुलाओ किसीको।' said Akhtar, throwing the rod on the carpet. Take him away. *Call somebody.*

One of the inmates runs for help.

It took around half an hour for the jail Medical Officer to arrive. He saw Bharat, who had fainted and his leg broken from below the knee. The swelling has reached a critical level.

It took nearly half an hour for the jail Medical Officer to arrive. By the time he arrived, Bharat lay unconscious on the cold floor, his leg twisted unnaturally below the knee. The skin around the injury was tight and discolored, the swelling having reached a dangerous level. The officer crouched down, inspecting the grotesque bulge of the fractured bone pressing against the flesh. He shook his head grimly.

'فوراً اس نوں خواجہ فرید دے کول منتقل کر دیو۔,' said the Medical Officer. *Immediately shift him to Khawaja Fareed.*

An ambulance, escorted by police, speeds toward Khawaja Fareed Hospital.

***

Khawaja Fareed Social Security Hospital.

Multan. Pakistan.

Amid the chaos, Khawaja Fareed Hospital struggles to cope with an unrelenting wave of casualties. A suicide bomber detonated himself during prayer at a nearby mosque, flooding the already overcrowded and understaffed hospital with critical patients. Sirens wail as ambulances, cars, and motorcycles jostle desperately to enter the jam-packed emergency area. Inside, pandemonium reigns. The corridors are teeming with frantic relatives and medical staff scrambling between the wounded. The emergency ward is a cacophony of screams, cries, and hurried orders, with stretchers, wheelchairs, and patients sprawled out on the floor, fighting for space and attention.

In one corner, a weary police constable fills out a registration form, his pen moving sluggishly through the paperwork. Beside him, another constable stands watch over a stretcher. Lying motionless on it is Bharat, still unconscious, his leg swollen and splinted. Amidst the turmoil, Mama Baloch, the male nurse assigned to Bharat.

Mama Baloch, a bulky fifty-year-old male nurse, has been a fixture at Khawaja Fareed Hospital for over two decades. His large hands, now accustomed to administering injections and tending to the wounded, once danced delicately over the strings of a *sarod*. In his youth, he was known throughout the Panjgur district as a musical prodigy, spending hours each day practicing with his elder brother, Bakhtawar. Together, their melodies were inseparable, and Bakhtawar's talent had earned him admission to the prestigious National Music Academy in Lahore.

But everything changed the day Bakhtawar disappeared. Without warning, his elder brother vanished from their home, leaving behind a silence that would forever haunt Mama Baloch. Deep in his heart, he knew the truth: the Pakistani army had taken Bakhtawar, like so many others in Balochistan. The fear of his family suffering the same fate gripped him, forcing him to flee his beloved Panjgur and settle in Multan.

'मामा इसको सेकंड फ्लोर OT में लेजाओ। जल्दी।' said the doctor, hurriedly. *Mama, take him to second floor OT. Fast.*

'ठीक है जनाब।' replied Mama, thrusting the file under Bharat's head. *Yes Sir.*

Mama Baloch's bulky frame moved with surprising agility, guiding the stretcher through the chaotic throngs. Years of navigating crowded emergency rooms had made him a master of the maze. With one hand firmly on the stretcher, he expertly weaved left and right, hackling and whistling loudly to part the sea of anxious relatives and hospital staff. Behind him, the two police constables struggled to keep up, their eyes darting warily around the bedlam.

'घबराओ नहीं जनाब. पोहोच जायेंगे।' said Mama, to police constable. *Don't worry sir. We will reach.*

'हां ठीक है चलो चलो।' said the police constable. *Yes yes. You keep pushing.*

As the lift doors creak open, Mama Baloch squeezes his way out, maneuvering through the press of people. With a furtive glance around, he slips his hand into his pocket and dials a number on his mobile phone. Moments later, the entire hospital plunges into darkness—a sudden, jarring blackout that silences the chatter and heightens the confusion. In the midst of the chaos, Mama moves with a grace to reach opertation theatre.

'जनाब आप इस वेटिंग रूम में ठहरो। अंदर आना मना है।' said Mama, pointing to the room in the right. *Sir you cannot come inside. You have to wait in this waiting room.*

'ठीक है,' said the police constable. *All right.*

After ensuring that Mama took Bharat into the operation theater, both the police constables walk inside the waiting room.

Mama's nephew, Anwar, is already waiting inside the anteroom with one patient. Anwar is also a male nurse.

'जल्दी करो मामा. डॉक्टर इंतजार कर रहा है,' said Anwar. *Hurry up, Mama. The doctor is waiting.*

'जनाब ओपेशन चल रहा है. हम इधर हि है. ऑपेरेशन थिएटर के सामने जनाब. आप चिंता ना करे,' said police constable on phone. *Yes, sir operation is going on. We both are here. In front of operation theater. You don't worry.*

Mama administers a quick Morphine shot to Bharat as Anwar drapes a *kafan*—a plain white shroud—over his limp body. Without missing a beat, Mama wheels Bharat out of the operation theater, concealed beneath the burial sheet. Meanwhile, Anwar guides the other patient in, slipping into the sterile room without a trace of hesitation.

With the lifts out of service, Mama opts for the ramp, pushing the stretcher steadily until he reaches the morgue on the ground floor. A handwritten sign on the door reads, "مردہ خانه بھرا ہوا ہے" (Morgue is full). Ignoring the warning, Mama presses forward and maneuvers Bharat inside.

The air is thick with the stench of decay, a suffocating odor that clings to everything. Inside, chaos reigns. Bodies are crammed together, piled haphazardly in every corner. Some have managed to find space on the overcrowded shelves, while others lie scattered across the floor, draped in stained sheets. The sight is grim—a landscape of death—but Mama navigates through the sea of lifeless forms, searching for a concealed spot among the mass of the deceased.

'मुस्तफा ये बॉडी किधर रखु?' said Mama, to morgue attendant. *Mustafa, where should I keep this body?*

'मामा जगा कहाँ है?' said Mustafa. *Mama, can't you see there is no place?*

'मुझे नहीं मालूम। मैं दरवाज़े पे रख के चला जाऊंगा।' said Mama, with anger. *I don't know all that. I will throw it on the door and go.*

'नाराज कियूं होते हो मामा? क्या नाम है?' said Mustafa. *Don't be angry Mama. What is the name?*

'लावारिस बोला है,' said Mama. *They said its unclaimed.*

'ईधी के कवर में डालके उधर ईधी वाले सेक्शन में रख दो,' said Mustafa. *Then put it in Edhi cover and keep in that Edhi section.*

Edhi Foundation, known for its compassionate work, plays a crucial role in handling unclaimed bodies from hospitals, ensuring they receive dignified burials. With a network of over six thousand volunteers across Pakistan, Edhi's presence is a lifeline for overcrowded hospitals like Khawaja Fareed.

Inside the morgue, Mama wraps Bharat carefully in an Edhi shroud, its white cloth emblazoned with the familiar logo. He makes tiny holes in the fabric for ventilation before placing Bharat among the other bodies in the designated Edhi section. He pauses, ensuring everything is in place, then steps back, his heart pounding lightly despite the calm exterior.

Exiting the morgue, Mama casts a discreet glance around before giving a subtle signal to the Edhi ambulance driver waiting nearby—a nondescript Suzuki van parked inconspicuously outside. The driver, Sambha, catches the sign immediately. Dressed in an oversized red t-shirt marked with the white 'Edhi' emblem on the back, he nods and steps out of the van, accompanied by two helpers similarly clad in Edhi uniforms. The three men enter the morgue.

'जल्दी चतले है। दूसरे हस्पताल भी तो जाना है।' said the driver to his helpers. *Let's go. We need to go to another hospital also.*

Sambha reach the Edhi section of the Morgue.

'हम ये चार लाशें ले जा रहे है,' informed driver to Mustafa. *We are taking these four bodies.*

'ठीक है भाई। और ये सब भी जल्दी से लेजाओ।' said Mustafa, pointing at other remaining corpses. *Ok brother. And also try to take all these bodies.*

'जनाब वहां खड़े हो कर देखनेसे से अच्छा है जरा हमे मदद करें।' said driver to Mama who is standing on the Morgue door. *Sir instead of standing there please come and help us.*

'जी जनाब माज़रत चाहता हूँ।' said Mama and rushed to the Edhi corner. *I am sorry.*

Mama grabs hold of Bharat's leg while Sambha secures his head. As the helpers focus on lifting the other unclaimed bodies, Mama and Sambha gently placing Bharat onto a stretcher and wheeling him out toward the van. They slide him under the rear seat, ensuring he is positioned safely away from where the other corpses will be stacked, protecting him from any accidental weight that might crush him. Once secured, they exchange a quick glance.

'अनवर को लेके चले जाओ शहर से,' said Sambha. *Take Anwar and leave the city.*

Mama felt an overwhelming urge to embrace the driver, but the situation held him back. Instead, he gave a subtle nod of gratitude. Meanwhile, Mustafa completed the formalities, taking the driver's signature before the van, now carrying four unclaimed bodies along with the two helpers, pulled away from the morgue.

Up on the second floor, however, tension is beginning to boil.

'ये तो डेड है हम क्या ऑपरेशन करेंगे? आप इसे ले जाओ। OT खली करना है दूसरे और भी इमरजेंसी पेशंटस इंतज़ार में है। जो भी करना है जल्दी कीजिये।' said doctor to police constables. *He is already dead. We cannot do anything. There are other emergency patients in line. Do whatever you want to do but do it fast. Please.*

'हम देख सकते है?' asked the Police constable. *Can we see?*

'Yes,' replied the doctor.

The constables stare in disbelief as they realize the lifeless figure on the operation theater bed isn't Bharat.

'वही कही ले गए होंगे उसको टेस्ट के लिए। जल्दीसे ढूंढो उसको। मैं आ रहा हूँ,' said the jailer on phone. *He must have been taken for some tests. You both immediately look around. I am coming there.*

***

Vahari – Multan Highway

The ambulance's high speed on the congested Vehari-Multan highway leaves both Edhi helpers shifting uneasily in their seats. Their discomfort deepens when, instead of continuing straight, the van suddenly takes a sharp U-turn at Vehari Chowk. The change in route is unexpected—unusual for a typical ambulance run. Yet, sensing the tension in the air, the helpers exchange wary glances but choose to stay silent.

***

Hotel Abu Bakar.

Muzaffargarh Highway. Pakistan.

The helpers' unease turns into fear as the ambulance speeds past the Bahawalpur bypass and veers onto the Muzaffargarh highway. This detour is far from standard, and they glance nervously at each other, the unfamiliar route deepening their suspicion.

'ये कहाँ ले जा रहे हो भाई? कुम्हारन वाला तो उस तरफ है।' said one helper, in panic. *Where are you taking us? Kumharan Wala is that side.*

The driver stops the van near Hotel Abu Bakar on Muzaffargarh road.

'भाई किसी को बताओगे तो नहीं।' said the driver. *Promise me that you will tell anybody.*

'क्या?' said one of the helpers. *What?*

'एक मेडिकल कॉलेज के साथ मैंने चार लाशों का सौदा किया है। ये डील नक्की होने के बाद और एडवांस पेमेंट लेने बाद ही मैंने ये ड्राइवर का काम उठाया। भाई अच्छे पैसे है इसमें। अगर आप मेरे साथ चलोगे तो आपको भी पैसे दूंगा। लावारिस लाशें है इसीलिए कोई खतरा नहीं है इसमें।' said the driver. *I have struck the deal of four dead bodies in a medical college. I will not tell you the name. First, they gave me advance money and helped me get this driver's job. There is good money in this. You will also get good money if you come along with me. And since these are unclaimed bodies, there is no risk.*

'पर भाई मुर्दाघर में अपने जिस कागज़ पर दस्तखत किये है उसमें साफ़ लिखा है की लाशें ईधी के कब्रस्तान में ले जायी जा

रही है। आप चुप चाप चलो कुम्हारन वाला। चलो भाई,' said helper. *But the Morgue paper which you have signed clearly says that the bodies will be taken to the registered Edhi graveyard. Just listen to us and let's hand over these bodies to Kumharan Wala graveyard.*

'भाई हम सब जानते है की कोई पढ़ेगा उस कागज को. और कोई नहीं पूछेगा इन लाशों को। वक़्त जाया ना करो और चलो,' said the driver. *Brother we all know that no comes to the graveyard to see these bodies. And no one checks that paper. Let's not waste the time.*

'नहीं भाई वापस चलो।' said the helper. *No let's go back.*

'जनाब मेडिकल कॉलेज में पढ़ाई के लिए ले जा रहा हूँ ये लाशें। और कोई मसला नहीं है इसमे।' said the driver. *I am taking these unclaimed bodies to medical college for study purpose. There is nothing more than that.*

The driver takes out fifty thousand rupees from his packet.

'ये एडवांस रखो। बाकि लाशें पोहोचने के बाद मिलेंगे। हम आपस में बांट लेंगे। चलो चलते है दूर जाना है।' said the driver, showing the money. *This is advance. And remaining money will be getting post-delivery. We will share equally. Let's go. Its far.*

'और अगर रेंजरों ने पकड़ा तो?' said the helper. *And if rangers catch us?*

'भाई ये ईधी की एम्बुलेंस है. कोई नहीं रोकता। हम ईधी है ईधी. आपको भी पता है. चलो।' said the driver. *It's Edhi. No one questions us. We are Edhi my brother. You also know. Let go.*

'नहीं हम नहीं आएंगे। तुम चोर हो।' said the helper. *No, we will not come with you. You are a smuggler.*

The driver gives money to one of the helpers. Helper takes it.

'ये अपना मुँह बंद रखने के लिए। बाट लेना आपस में। घर जाओ रिक्शा से। और याद रखो इसमें कोई भी गलत काम नहीं है। खुदा हाफिस।' said the driver. *This is for keeping your mouth shut. Distribute equally between both of you. Don't worry. I remember that there is nothing wrong in this. Go home by rickshaw. Khuda Afis.*

Both the helpers step out and close the door. With a low rumble, the van pulls away, merging smoothly onto the Muzaffargarh highway and picking up speed as it glides along the road, its destination shrouded in silence.

***

Garbage Pit.

Muzaffargarh Highway. Pakistan.

Sambha halts the ambulance beside a desolate roadside garbage pit and, heaves the three bodies into the pile of refuse. Afterward, he pulls off the plastic cover shielding Bharat. Bharat lies motionless, unconscious, his leg badly swollen. With a quick glance around, Sambha retrieves his mobile phone and tosses it into the pit, severing the last link to their trail.

Turning back, he grabs a sterile fluids bag, sets up the IV line (therapy), and inserts the needle into Bharat's arm. Within moments, the clear liquid begins to flow steadily into his veins.

'अय भरत्या? सगळा पायच मोडून टाकला व्हय? अक्कल हे का तुला कही? आरामशनको घेऊ. आरामशीर तुला आपल्या मातीत घेऊन जातो का नही बघ. हे कहीच नही. महाराज आगऱ्या ऊन आले होते. आरामशीर चलत चलत. यांच्या आयला यांच्या। आपुन कधी भी हनुन काढू यान्ह्रा. हर हर महादेव। हर हर महादेव,' said Sambha to the Bharat who is sleeping unconsciously. *Bhartya? Who told you to break the entire leg? Don't worry now. Just see how I take you to our mother land comfortably. This mission is nothing as compare to what our Maharaj use to do. How easily our Maharaj had returned from Agra. You just relax. Har Har Mahadev. Har Har Mahadev.*

Once assured that Bharat is stable, the van resumes its journey. Sambha drives relentlessly, eyes fixed on the road, unwavering for hours as the day slowly melts away. The harsh white sky softens into a warm crimson, and the sun casts long, stretching shadows over the empty highway. As dusk settles in, he spots a signboard up ahead: *'Kabir Wala 60 Km.'*

Glancing at it, Sambha quickly pulls out his satellite phone to double-check the route. With a confirming nod, he takes a sharp left, steering the van toward Kabir Wala as the evening light deepens around him.

'जनाब गोश ले लिया है मैंने। अब रास्ते में डेकोरेशन वाले के पास पहुंचकर काल करता हूँ।' said Sambha on satellite phone. *Sir, I have purchased meat. Now, I will give you a call on I reached the decoration shop.*

***

Bahirji Complex.

India.

Patil sits alone in the quiet cabin of the Bahirji Complex. He sets the phone down and glances up at the wall clock. It reads 19:10 hours in India.

'बारा तास लागतेन रोड नि,' said Patil to himself. *It will take at least twelve hours by road.*

He slams the table and walks out of the cabin.

The video wall inside the control and command room of Bahirji Complex is displaying Pakistan's territory map. A small red dot is blinking on Kabirwala road. The dot is Sambha.

'एकोनतीस किलोमीटर आहे फाइजाबाद पासून,' said Bahirji operator. *Twenty-nine kilometers away from Faisalabad.*

'We have activated our assets,' said Sandeep.

***

Khawaja Fareed Hospital,

Multan. Pakistan.

The jailer is interrogating his police constables.

'मुझे सच बचाओ. कितिने पैसे मिले है तुम दोनो को?' asked the jailer. *Tell me the truth. How much money you got for this?*

'जनाब हमे कूच पता नाही है आप क्या केह रहे है . हम दोनो खुद ऊस स्ट्रेचर के साथ आये थे. उस स्ट्रेचर पर भरत हि था. अलाह कसम,' said the police constable who is sitting on the chair. *Sir, we have no idea what you are talking about. We both personally walked with the stretcher on which Bharat was lying. Swear to Allah.*

'और फीर वो गायब हो गया? हवा मी. मुझे बेवकूफ मत बनावो। अब मुझे ऊपर बताना होगा। ,' said the jailer, taking out his mobile and dialing. *And then what happened? Bharat disappeared? You are fooling me. I must inform this to the higher authority.*

***

Garbage Pit.

Muzaffargarh Highway. Pakistan.

By the side of the Muzaffargarh highway, Hamid examines the bodies pulled from the pit. Nearby, a senior police officer holds up photographs, questioning the detained Edhi helpers who were in the ambulance.

'अगर इसकी लम्बी दाढ़ी हटा दी जाये तो जनाब उस ड्राइवर की तरह दिखेगा।' said one of the helpers, pointing at the photograph. *If you remove his long beard he will look like that driver.*

'इस तरफ गया था वह सीधा। बोल रहा था दूर जाना है,' said the other helper. *He went straight in this direction. He was telling us that medical college is far away.*

'कराची. या गवादर. ऐसा कुछ कहा था क्या उसने?' asked Hamid from behind. *Has he said anything like Karachi or Gawadar?*

'नहीं जनाब पर इस तरफ दूर जाने की बात कर रहा था।' said the helper. *No Sir. But he was saying that he has to go very far.*

'Sir, I think he will follow the Kasab route,' said the police officer to Hamid.

Hamid remains silent, his expression unreadable as he stares steadily at the highway. He knows this road runs straight south, all the way to the Arabian Sea. In his mind, he can already hear the distant roar of its restless waves, carrying Bharat away from him, making him further restless.

'तुम पेहेले लाशों की टांगे चेक करो।' said Hamid. *You first find the body with a broken leg.*

***

ISI Control Room.

Rawalpindi. Pakistan.

The video wall in the control room displays a sprawling map of Pakistan, with Quetta and Karachi prominently highlighted. Regions are marked according to their alert levels, the map dotted with red and orange circles, indicating areas of high and moderate risk. Most of the country is covered in a mosaic of warning colors.

'वो ये लम्बा रास्ता लेगा। किसी भी और रास्ते के मुकाबले ये रास्ता सेफ है उसके लिए। जेट्टी तक पोहोंचने से पहले ही उसे इंटरसेप्ट करना होगा। सुक्कुर, लरकाना,खैरपुर, नवाबशाह। यही कहीं उसको रोक लेंगे। हैदराबाद नहीं पोहोंचना चाहिए वो।' said Hamid, dragging the stick from Multan to the Karachi coast. *He will take a long route. It is safe for him as compared to other routes. We will have to intercept him well before he reaches the coast. Sukkur, Larkana, Khairpun, Nawabshah. These are the areas where we have to focus. He should not reach Hyderabad.*

'Put everybody on high alert,' said Hamid.

'Yes sir,' said the operator.

A deluge of information streams into the control room as reports flood in from the field. Across Quetta and Karachi, officers in plain clothes are stopping civilians for questioning, frisking them. Temporary barricades have sprung up on major routes, choking the flow of traffic. Highways NH5, NH55, and motorways M5 and M4 are heavily congested, the increased security slowing movement to a crawl. The atmosphere is tense, with checkpoints and roadblocks becoming chokepoints in an urgent hunt.

***

Chaudhri Guesthouse.

Gojra. Pakistan.

The night is young as the ambulance finally pulls up at Chaudhari Guest House on the outskirts of Gojra. Dressed in a black *salwar kurta* and a traditional Sindhi *Topi*, Sambha steps out, now disguised as a cloth merchant. He strides confidently into the guest house.

The entrance lobby is small and dimly lit, with only a faint buzz of activity. Behind the reception desk, a boy no older than fifteen lounges in a worn chair, engrossed in his mobile phone. His eyes barely flicker up as Sambha approaches, his attention fixed on the screen.

'सलाम वालेकुम,' said Sambha. *Hello.*

'सलाम,' said the receptionist. *Hello.*

'मुस्तफा भाई कौनसे कमरे में है?' asked Sambha. *Which one is Mustafa's room?*

'ऊपर. 03,' answered the boy. *03. Upstairs.*

Sambha casts a wary glance over his shoulder at the boy still absorbed in his phone. Something about him feels off, sparking a flicker of doubt in Sambha's mind. Without drawing attention, he quietly turns and makes his way up the stairs.

Reaching room number 03, he pauses and raps softly on the door. The sound is answered almost immediately as the door swings open. Standing there is Mustafa.

'सामान तैयार है?' asked Sambha, entering hurriedly. *Is everything ready?*

'हाँ जनाब रस्ते में है। बस दस आता ही होगा. आप आराम फरमाए।' said Mustafa, shrugging his beefy shoulders. *Yes, sir. It is on the way. Should be coming shortly. You take some rest.*

As Sambha sits on the edge of the bed, the receptionist downstairs is already on the phone, speaking in hushed tones.

'जनाब शायद वो आया है।' said the receptionist on the phone. *Sir, I think that he is here.*

***

ISI Control Room.

Rawalpindi. Pakistan.

Hamid and Major Fawad are listening on the speakerphone.

'तुम नज़र रखो उस पर।' said Hamid. *Ok. You keep an eye on him.*

'ठीक है जनाब।' said the receptionist. Hamid cuts the call. *Ok. Sir.*

'असाल्ट टीम भेजो।' said Hamid to the operator. *Send the assault team.*

'जनाब।' said operator. *Yes Sir.*

'क्या लग रहा है?' asked Fawad. *What do you say, Sir?*

'ये बस एक लीड है फवाद।' said Hamid. *It's just one of the many leads.*

Hamid looks at the map of southern highways of Pakistan.

'सर हम ऊपर वाले हाईवे पर भी अलर्ट भेज दे?' said Fawad. *Shall we send an alert to the northern routes?*

This is an important tactical question. Hamid takes his time to answer. Hamid walks closer to the map. With the pointer, he points at the locations: Faisalabad, Lahore, Islamabad, and Rawalpindi.

'मैं हिन्दुस्तानियों को जनता हूँ. वो ये रास्ता नहीं लेगा। फैसलाबाद, रावलपिंडी, लाहौर, इस्लामाबाद, ये सब क्रॉस करना नामुमकिन है। तुम्हे क्या लगता है।' asked Hamid. *I know Indians. I don't think he will take this northern route. Able to cross Faisalabad, Rawalpindi, Islamabad, Lahore is out of the question. This is out of the question. What do you say?*

'हाँ सर ये रास्ता बोहोत सिक्योर है और लम्बा भी है। खुद ख़ुशी नहीं करेगा वो।' said Fawad. *You are right sir. It's a very secure and long route. He will not take that risk.*

Hamid again points to the locations: Dera Ismail Khan, Kohat, Mianwali, Peshawar, Landi Kotal, and Torkham.

'यहाँ डेरा इस्माइल, पेशावर के रस्ते तोरखम बॉर्डर से निकलना मुश्किल है पर नामुमकिन नहीं है. वो जा सकता है।' said Hamid. *Taking the Dera Ismail Khan, Peshawar and escaping from Torkham border crossing can be a tough choice. But not an impossible one. He can go.*

'इस एरिया में खासकर लण्डी कोतल और तोरखम के आस पास हिंदुस्तानी एसेट्स का नेटवर्क मजबूत है।' said Fawad. *Indian assets have their presence in these areas. Especially in Landi Kotal, Torkham areas.*

'उसके साथ एक क्याज़ुलटी भी है।' said Hamid. *Remember there is a casualty with him.*

Hamid hovers the pointer over the locations: Hyderabad, Mirpur Khas, Umarkot.

'कोस्ट तक पहुंचने के लिए हैदराबाद, मीरपुर खास, उमरकोट, पंजगुर , ये उसके लिए आसान रास्ते है। यहाँ की गैरकानूनी जेट्टियों से दुश्मन अच्छि तरह से वाकिफ है। ग्वादर, पसनी , ओरमरा, कुंद मलीर, इनमेसे कोई भी उसके लिए ट्रांजिट पॉइंट

बन सकता है।' said Hamid. *It is easy for him to use any of these routes: Hyderabad, Mirpur Khas, Umarkot, Khuzdar, Panjgur. To reach these coastal areas. The enemy knows that there are many unofficial jetties on the coastline. Gwadar, Pasni, Ormara, Kund Malir, any of these could be having a possible transit jetty. It's a porous maritime border.*

'जी जनाब।' said Fawad. *Yes Sir.*

'दुश्मन चाहता है कि हम अपने वसाइल हर जगह तैनात करें। अभी अगर हम और इलाकों में अलर्ट भेजने तो पुरे देश खलबली मचेगी। कोस्ट गार्ड को भी अभी इन्फॉर्म नहीं करते है. गोजरा से कन्फर्मेशन का इंतज़ार करते है।' said Hamid. *Hmm, the enemy wants to deploy our resources all over the places. Sending an alert to the other areas will create a national-level panic. Don't inform coast guard now. Let's wait for the confirmation from Gojra.*

***

Chaudhary Guesthouse.

Gojra. Pakistan.

Sambha's expression tightens with this uncessary delay.

'बोहोत देर नहीं हो गयी?' asked Sambha, sitting on the sofa. *Don't you think it's too late?*

Sambha grabs the water bottle from the side table but doesn't drink.

'सब जगह नाका बंदी है। कोई खास वजस पता नहीं चली अभी तक। मुल्तान में हुए मस्जिद ब्लास्ट की वजह से ये नाकाबंदी है शायद।' said Mustafa, smoking *Shisha*. *Yes. police checking is going in all the corners. No one is telling the real reason but I think it's because of the Masjid blast in Multan.*

'मैं तो मंडी में था दिन भर। सारा सामान लिया। मुल्तान ही पोहोंचना है फज्र से पहले।' said Sambha, sitting on the sofa. *Whole day I was in the wholesale market. Did some shopping. I have to reach Multan before Fajr.*

Sambha surfs TV channels. Mustafa is smoking *Shisha*.

The assault team arrives at Chaudhri Guest House, moving silently. Pistols and knives secured in holsters, rifles slung over their shoulders, they are a formidable sight in their bulletproof jackets. The team stands poised, ready for the raid.

'फिरसे देख लो फोटो को। सिविलियन एक भी मरना नहीं चाहिए। एकदम क्लीन और साइलेंट ऑपरेशन होना चाहिए।' said Rashid, team leader. *See the photograph once again. Not a single civilian should be killed. This has to be a clean and quiet operation.*

The team comes out of the car. Rashid immediately dials the phone.

'शमशाद क्या पोजीशन है?' asked Rashid, on phone. *What is the position Shamshad?*

'मै बालकनी के दरवाज़े से देख सकता हूँ| वो टीवी देख रहा है। सिर्फ चैनल ही बदल रहा है। मेंन दरवाज़े के ठीक सामने जो सोफा है, बालकनी की दिवार को सट के, वो वहीँ बैठा है। शीशा पि रहा होगा। धुंआ ज्यादा है।' said Shamshad. *I can see from the balcony door that he is watching TV or rather just surfing the channels. He is sitting on the sofa that is exactly in front of the main door. The one which is along the balcony wall. He must be smoking Sheesha.*

Shamshad steadies his rifle on the parapet wall of the adjacent house, his gaze fixed through the riflescope. The crosshairs align perfectly as he peers into the room—a haze of smoke lingers in the air, and the TV screen flickers with shifting channels, casting fleeting shadows across the walls.

A former state-level shooting champion, Shamshad's skill is unmatched. But the thrill of medals and applause has long faded. Now, he trades life for profit. His target today will earn him a hefty sum, paid in crisp dollars directly to his Dubai account. A silent killer with unerring aim, he is a man driven not by the hunt, but by the price on his prey.

'और मुस्तफा है?' asked Rashid. *Can you Mustafa?*

'उधर ही होगा । क्यूंकि बाकि मूवमेंट नज़र नहीं आ रही है।' said Shamshad. *Must be smoking Shisha. Because there is no other movement.*

'मुस्तफा भी अंदर है। उसको बचाके।' Rashid keeps his mobile phone back in his pocket and leads the team to the main gate. *Mustafa is inside. Don't shoot him.*

The assault team takes the position in front of room number 03. Rashid is pointing his AK 47 at the door. He takes out his phone.

'कोई खबर?' asked Rashid. *Any movement?*

'कोई मूवमेंट नहीं है। बस टीवी चैनल बदले जा रहे है। नशा कर रहे है शायद।' said Shamshad. *No. He is just changing TV channels. They must be high.*

'ओके. हम अन्दर दाखिल हो रहे है। खुदा हाफिस।' said Rashid. *OK. We are going.*

'खुदा हासिद,' said Shamshad. *All right.*

One of the team members slots the key into the lock and turns it. The door clicks open, and Rashid charges in, delivering a powerful kick that sends it swinging wide as he moves into position inside the hall. He scans the room quickly, eyes darting over every corner.

But the hall is empty.

Dead Mustafa slump on the sofa, his head tilted at an unnatural angle. A thin plume of smoke rises from the Shisha, the slow-burning coal crackling softly on the foil. The air is heavy with the scent of tobacco. Rashid signals to his team, who fan out, checking the bathroom, toilet, and balcony in quick succession. All clear. No signs of life.

Rashid's gaze shifts to the side table. A smartphone rests there, its screen dark. He picks it up, glancing at the blank display.

'यहां से चैनल बदल रहा है,' said Rashid. *Channel is changing from here.*

Rashid slams the phone on the floor, breaking it into pieces.

Let's rewind the clock by half an hour—Sambha and Mustafa sit in silence.

'कॉल करो और देखो क्या बात है।' said Sambha, walking to the balcony. *Make a call and check what is the status.*

'अभी करता हूँ।' said Mustafa. *Yes. I will call and check.*

Sambha's eyes narrow as they settle on a drainage pipe running along the edge of the balcony. He reaches out and gives it a firm push, testing its strength. The pipe holds steady. Good. It's solid enough to bear his weight if needed. He steps back, his gaze sweeping the area below.

Across the road, a similar bungalow stands shrouded in darkness. To its side, a long, narrow alley stretches into the shadows, cloaked in obscurity—an ideal escape route. Sambha's mind works quickly, mapping out possible moves and exits.

'सुनो मुझे तुम्हे जिन्दा पकड़ने का हुक्म मिला है। तुम चुचाप अंदर आओ और सोफे पर बैठ जाओ।' said Mustafa, standing at the balcony door and pointing a pistol at Sambha. *Listen, I got the orders to catch you alive. So please come inside and sit on the sofa.*

It is a SIG Sauer compact pistol used mainly by Pakistani special forces.

'ये क्या कर रहे तुम? मैं आप में से ही तो एक हूँ। खुदा के लिए ये बन्दुक निचे रखो। मुझे बोहोत डर लगता है। मेरे घरवाले मुल्तान में मेरी राह देख रहे होंगे। छोटे छोटे बच्चे है मेरे।' said Sambha. *What are you doing my brother? You are mistaken. Put that gun down. I am one of you, my brother. For God's sake don't shoot. I have my family waiting in Multan.*

'तुम मेरी बात मनो और चुपचाप अंदर आ जाओ,' said Mustafa. *Listen to me. Get inside.*

'मुझे मारों मत। जरूर कोई गलती हुई तुमसे। बैठ के बातें करते है।' said Sambha. *Don't shoot my brother don't shoot. You are mistaken. I will sit. Let us talk.*

Sambha steps cautiously into the room, his movements slow and deliberate as his eyes lock onto Mustafa. But before he can fully enter, Mustafa raises a pistol, the barrel aimed squarely at Sambha's chest.

Then, like lightning, Sambha reacts. In one fluid motion, he ducks beneath the gun's aim, closing the gap between them and pulling Mustafa's arm tight against his own body. Mustafa's eyes widen in shock, but it's too late. Sambha twists his wrist sharply, the pistol slipping free into his hand. Before Mustafa can recover, Sambha drives his elbow hard into his face, sending him staggering back, blood spurting from his nose.

Sambha takes a step back, his stance steady as he levels the gun at Mustafa, who is now stumbling near the doorway, disoriented and struggling to stay upright. Without a moment's hesitation, Sambha squeezes the trigger—BOOM! BOOM! The gunshots ring out, precise and unforgiving. Two clean headshots tear through Mustafa's skull, and his body crumples lifelessly to the floor.

'हर हर महादेव,' said Sambha, panting. *Har Har Mahadev.*

Sambha drags Mustafa onto the sofa and rifles through his pockets until his fingers close around a set of car keys—Toyota keys. He glances around, then sets his plan into motion. Connecting the TV to a custom mobile app, he places the phone inconspicuously on the side table. The Shisha still smolders softly as he arranges the burning charcoal on the silver foil, the smoke adding an air of casualness to the setup.

Without wasting another second, Sambha slips onto the balcony and clambers down the drainage pipe, moving with the agility of a cat. He drops silently into the narrow alley below, melting into the shadows. Just a few paces away, a lone Toyota Hilux stands parked—the only Toyota in sight. Sambha unlocks the vehicle, slides behind the wheel, and starts the engine. The sound is muted against the thick night air as he maneuvers the Hilux out of the alley.

Sambha drives, navigating through back streets until he reaches a secluded, pitch-dark corner where the ambulance is hidden. He pulls up beside it and quickly gets to work. He transfers Bharat—still unconscious, with the saline drip intact—into the back of the Hilux, securing him safely. Once everything is set, Sambha climbs back into the driver's seat and accelerates onto the Multan–Faisalabad Motorway, disappearing into the night with Bharat and the mission intact.

***

Pindi Bhattian.

Islamabad – Lahore Motorway. Pakistan.

At Pindi Bhattian, the Hilux veered left, merging onto the Islamabad-Lahore Motorway. Originally, Sambha's goal at the Chaudhary Guest House had been twofold: securing the Hilux and retrieving a bag of cash. While the money had slipped through his fingers, driving away in the sturdy Hilux was at least a partial win.

***

ISI Control Room

Rawalpindi. Pakistan.

Hamid on speakerphone.

'कोई क्याजुलटी?' asked Hamid. *Any casualty?*

'जनाब एक एजेंट शहीद हो गया है।' said Rashid. *Sir, our agent got killed in this operation.*

CCTV footage flashes on the LED screen. It's Sambha running from the Guest House.

'ये वही संभा है जिसने हमारे लड़कों को मारा था पुणे में।' said Fawad. *He is the same officer who had planned the killings of our boys in Pune.*

Hamid is shocked to see Sambha.

'तुम गोजरा को सील करो। ढूंढो उसे,' said Hamid. *You seal Gojra and search him.*

'गोजरा को सील करो। सर्वेलन्स लेवल हायस्ट करो।' said Hamid. *Seal Gojra. Increase the surveillance level to the highest.*

'जी जनाब।' said the operator. *Yes, Sir.*

On the video wall, new red circles start flashing. These are mostly around the Gojra.

In space, the Pakistani satellite is shifting its axis. Drones are flying over Gojra.

***

Islamabad – Lahore Motorway.

Pakistan.

The Hilux rattles along the dark, uneven road, its headlights piercing through clouds of dust swirling in the night air. The rough terrain jostles the vehicle, but Sambha keeps a steady grip on the wheel, his gaze fixed on the desolate path ahead. In the backseat, Bharat lies motionless, still unconscious, his leg swollen and bandaged.

Sambha remains silent, lost in thought as the vehicle lumbers forward into the darkness.

***

Multan Central Jail.

Multan. Pakistan.

It's a dark room. Two ISI officers are slapping and hitting the jailer.

***

Islamabad – Lahore Motorway.

Hilux is running. Sambha dials his satellite phone.

***

ISI Control Room.

Rawalpindi. Pakistan.

An alert is flashing on the video wall of the control room. The location is somewhere on Lahore-Islamabad highway.

'जनाब दुश्मन की लाइन मिल गयी।' said the operator. *Sir, there is voice transmission on the enemy channel.*

Hamid and Fawad walks to the phone and turns on the speakers.

'जनाब कब करना है बिस्मिल्लाह। मेरे लड़के मार्च के लिए तैयार है।' the phone conversation. *Sir, my boys are ready. Tell us when we should join the march. Sir, can you hear me?*

***

Bahirji Complex.

India.

Inside the control room at Bahirji, Patil does not answer because he can see a communication warning signal flashing.

'आपली लाईन इंतरसेप्ट केली आहे त्यांही,' informed operator to Patil. *They have intercepted our lines.*

'आपको किस से बात करनी है? ये रॉंग नंबर है।' said Patil to Sambha, disconnecting the phone in desperation. *With whom do you want to talk? It's a wrong number do not disturb.*

'आपल्या लाईनस कस्काय ब्रीच झाल्या?' shouted Patil with great anger. *How can they enter into our communication?*

Patil bangs the table.

***

Islamabad – Lahore Motorway.

Realizing there's been a breach in the communication line, Sambha immediately pulls the car to a stop. He dismantles the satellite phone piece by piece, tossing the components in different directions into the surrounding darkness. With a deep breath, he pulls out a folded map, spreading it open under the dim glow of the dashboard light.

His eyes flicker over the crisscrossed routes, analyzing every detail. One path leads west, cutting through Rawalpindi and heading toward Torkham at the Afghan border. The other veers east, winding through Rawalpindi toward the rugged terrain of Abbottabad. He weighs his options carefully, knowing that every turn could decide their fate.

***

Muzaffarabad
Abbottabad
Chakoti
Torkham Border
Afghanistan
Rawalpindi
Lahore - Islamabad Motorway
Lahore
Multan
Bharat
Karachi Port

ISI Control Room

Rawalpindi. Pakistan.

On the video wall, the blinking cursor that had been tracking Sambha's every move suddenly vanishes, leaving only a static map.

'सिग्नल लॉस हो गया सर।' said the operator. *We lost him.*

Eyes widen around the control room as the realization sinks in—Sambha has slipped off their radar.

'मैसेज डिकोड करो।' said Hamid. *Decode the message.*

'जी जनाब।' said Fawad. *Yes Sir.*

***

Katchery Bazaar, Faisalabad.

Pakistan

On the bustling streets of Faisalabad, the hunt is on. Hundreds of police officers are stationed at every intersection, scanning the faces of passersby and scrutinizing vehicles inching through the traffic.

***

ISI Control Room

Rawalpindi. Pakistan.

The operator strides over to Hamid and hands him a slip of paper. Hamid's eyes narrow as he reads the decoded message: *Fiza Logistics.* Without a word, he turns sharply and moves toward the video wall, his gaze zeroing in on the Torkham border crossing. He raises a finger, pointing at the map's flashing indicator.

Fawad, sensing the urgency, steps up beside him. The clock is ticking, and every second counts.

'ये अफ़ग़ानिस्तान में है। तोरखम बॉर्डर पर।' said Hamid. *This is in Afghanistan. On the Torkham border.*

'अफ़ग़ान इंटेलिजेन्स उनके साथ में है।' said Fawad. *Afghan intelligence is with them.*

'बिकुल,' said Hamid. *Off course.*

Hamid's mind is focused on the map. He is hovering the pointer on the Torkham and Peshawar highway. Hamid is thinking.

'सिर्फ ये GT रोड ही जो उसे तोरखम तक पहुंचा सकता है।' said Hamid. *The only way to reach Torkham is this GT road.*

'पर जनाब GT तो जाम है। वहां पिछले दो दिनों से मौलाना का मिलेनियम मार्च चल रहा है।' said Fawad. *But Sir, GT road is completely jammed. Maulana's Millennium March has been going on since the last couple of days.*

'हाँ मेजर। बात तो सही है तुम्हारी। पर मुझे लगता है की इस GT रोड को दुश्मन ने अपने लिए सेफ पैसेज बना लीया है। आखिर मौलाना भी तो एक सियासतदान है।' said Hamid. *Yes. Fawad Yes. You are right. But I think the enemy has made this GT road a safe passage. After all, Maulana is also a politician.*

'जनाब मुझे इजाज़त दे. मैं खुद मौलाना को पकड़के यहाँ हाज़िर करता हूँ।' said Fawad, with great anger. *Sir, let me go and arrest Maulana with my own hands.*

'नहीं। उन्हें शक हो जायेगा। मौलाना के मार्च को चलने दो. हमे पेशावर पोहोचने से पेहेले ही उसे पकड़ना होगा।' said Hamid. *No. It will alert him. Let Maulana protest. We will have to catch him even before he reaches Peshawar.*

***

Kot Momin.

Islamabad – Lahore Motorway. Pakistan.

Questions swirl in Sambha's mind, relentless and unyielding: *Will there be an army check post up ahead? Is someone tailing me? Why is that man staring at me? Am I heading in the right direction? Will Bharat survive? Is he still breathing?* And then the deeper pangs of uncertainty hit—*Where is Sarah? Where is the hill?*

Navigating through the hostile terrain of his thoughts, Sambha grips the wheel tighter, pushing forward along the Lahore-Islamabad highway. The darkness outside mirrors his turmoil within. Just before reaching Kot Momin, his eyes catch a faint glimmer on a distant hill—a cluster of three small green bulbs blinking softly against the night.

Relief floods his chest. It's the sign he's been searching for—the signal of safety. Without hesitation, Sambha veers off the highway, guiding the Hilux onto a narrow dirt path leading to the hill. Gravel crunches beneath the tires as he pulls up at the foothill, finally parking the vehicle under the shadow of the looming hillside. For a moment, the world seems to pause. He's made it. For now.

Sambha quietly steps out of the driver's seat and moves to the back of the Hilux. Leaning inside, he gazes down at Bharat, his face etched with concern. Gently, he tilts Bharat's head, trickling a few drops of water into his parched mouth. The unconscious man's lips barely respond, but Sambha persists, ensuring he swallows.

Then, he prepares another dose of morphine and injects it swiftly. His eyes narrow as he notices the swelling around the original drip needle caused by the jarring journey over rough terrain. Without a second thought, Sambha removes the needle, finding a fresh spot on Bharat's other hand. He inserts it deftly, securing the IV line before checking the flow.

For a brief moment, Sambha's hardened demeanor softens. He places a hand on Bharat's forehead, feeling the clammy warmth. His brow furrows, a flicker of worry passing through him. But there's no time to dwell on it. They're not safe yet.

'Don't worry I will take you safely, directly to Maharaj, to Raigarh. That's my job,' said Sambha, in his shaky voice.

Sambha steps out of the Hilux and sinks to the ground, leaning against the rear tire. Exhaustion wraps around him like a thick blanket. He pulls out a chocolate bar from his pocket, savoring each bite in the cold night air. The darkness is dense and still, pressing in on him. For the first time, he is feeling lonely. His world is falling away, leaving him alone with his thoughts.

Something cracks within. Sambha's grip loosens, and the half-eaten chocolate bar slips from his fingers. The tears come unbidden, spilling over his cheeks as he doubles over, his shoulders shaking with silent sobs. He weeps uncontrollably, emotion pouring out—grief, fear, anger—all that he has buried deep inside. The sound of his tears echoes softly in the empty night. He doesn't fight it. He lets it all out, feeling his pain bleed into the silence around him.

When the tears finally subside, he feels an inexplicable lightness, a strange sense of calm settling over him. He sits there, drained and bewildered, almost in disbelief that he could cry at all. Why? What triggered it? He searches his mind but finds no answers. Instead, he shakes his head, lost in thought, and spots the chocolate wrapper lying beside him.

He picks up the torn wrapper. The orange and white glint faintly under the moonlight. He begins to tear the wrapper into pieces. First, he lays down the orange piece, then places the white one below it. He pauses, then reaches out, plucking a single blade of grass and positioning it under the white piece. Finally, he gathers a few tiny bits of gravel and places them at the center of the white strip.

He leans back and gazes at what he has created— a tiny tricolor, India's flag, arranged on Pakistani soil. A small, defiant smile spreads across his tear-streaked face, his eyes shining with a mix of pride and bittersweet joy. With emotion still thick in his throat, he begins to hum softly, then whispers the lyrics of an Indian Army Marching song:

‘तू शेर ए हिन्द आगे बढ़

मरने से तू कभी ना डर

उड़ा के दुश्मनों का सर

जोश ए वतन बढ़ाये जा

कदम कदम बढ़ाए जा

खुशी के गीत गाए जा’

A sudden gust of cool wind brushes against his face, carrying with it a fleeting sense of freedom.

'हे काहीच नाही. महाराज आगन्या ऊन आले होते. आरामशीर चलत चलत. मि भरतला घेऊन जाणार म्हणजे जाणार,' whispers Sambha, to himself. *This is nothing. How easily our Maharaj had returned from Agra. I will also take Bharat to India.*

Sambha is back with all his energies restored. He wipes his tears, gets up, and walks down the hill, leaving Bharat in the car.

***

Kot Momin Village.

Pakistan.

Sambha moves cautiously through the darkness, his eyes scanning the quiet foothill village. The silhouettes of mud houses blur together in the night, making it difficult to distinguish one from the other.

He slows his pace, taking his time as he studies each structure, searching for the one he remembers.

Finally, his gaze lands on a small mud house nestled beside an old mango tree. Standing before the door, he knocks four times in quick succession—thak thak thak thak—a secret code shared only by those who know what it means.

'कौन है आप?' asked a woman from inside. *Who are you?*

'दरवाज़ा खोलो भाई चाचा हूँ चाचा। तुम्हारा चाचा,' said Sambha in a low voice. *Open the door. I am your uncle. I am your uncle.*

'इतना वक़्त कैसे लगा?' said woman. *Why are you so late?*

'मग़रिब के बाद गाड़ी मिलना मुश्किल हो गया था।' said Sambha. *It was difficult to get transport after the Maghrib.*

The door creaks open, revealing Sarah standing quietly in a black hijab. Without a word, he slips into the small, dimly lit room and glances around. In one corner, a few essential items lie scattered on the bed—a sack, a pistol, and boxes of ammunition. Sambha wastes no time. He reaches into the sack and pulls out a fake black-and-white beard and mustache set. With deft hands, he begins attaching them to his face, using the small mirror propped against the wall to check his work.

'आपल्या सगळ्या लाईन्स हॅक केले त्यांही,' said Saraha. *They hacked our communication lines.*

'मी फोन फेकून दिला. बिलाल कुठंय?' said Sambha. *I threw my phone. Where is Bilal?*

'अजून नाही पोहोचला. सगळीकडं पोलीस आहेत,' said Sahar, sitting on the bed. *Not yet reached. He must be stuck in the market because of heavy police deployment.*

'ते आपली सगळी मुव्हमेंट ट्रॅक करत आहेत,' said Sarah. *They are monitoring all the movements.*

Sambha turns his hair into gray-black and wears a loose black kurta-pajama. His gaze shifts to the bed, lingering briefly on the scattered gear. Bilal is nowhere to be seen, and patience is no longer an option. With a decisive look, Sambha reaches for a couple of Glock magazines, loading them into the holster strapped to his waist. It's time to move forward, with or without Bilal.

'सर बिलाल ची इंटेल यउस्तर थांबलं पाहिजे. नवीन सॅटेलाईट फोन पण आणणार आहे तो,' said Sarah. *Sir, shall we wait for Bilal's intel? He is also going to arrange new satellite phones.*

Sambha attaches the suppressor to the pistol, the metal clicking softly as it locks into place. He slides the weapon back into the thigh holster. Then, he picks up a gray blanket from the bed and wraps it tightly around his shoulders.

'तू पार्सल ची काळजी घे . मी बिलाल ला बघतो,' said Sambha. *You take care of the parcel. I will see Bilal later.*

'एस सर,' said Sarah. Yes Sir.

Sambha walks out of the house. Sarah follows.

It's a blue police van parked behind the house. Sambha opens its door.

Sarah interrupts.

'सर?' said Sarah, extending her right hand. *Sir?*

'रायगडावर भेटू,' said Sarah. *See you at Raigarh.*

'रायगडावर भेटू,' said Sambha. *See you at Raigarh.*

'Yes,' said Sambha, shaking hand.

Sambha gets into the driver's seat and drives away. He is back on Islamabad – Lahore Motorway.

***

Islamabad – Lahore Motorway.

Pakistan.

Sambha, disguised as a police driver, confidently drives the police van toward Rawalpindi. Big 'On Special Duty' sticker glued on the windshield.

***

Bhalwal – Kot Momin Road.

Pakistan.

Draped in a burka, Sarah drives the Hilux steadily through the remote hinterland roads, choosing this hidden path to transport Bharat safely to the designated safe house. The night hums with a strange alertness, every shadow seeming alive as she navigates the treacherous terrain under the cover of darkness.

***

Grand Trunk Road.

Pakistan.

It's nine in the morning, and the Grand Trunk (GT) Road is swarming with a sea of five to six thousand party workers. Clad in bright orange skull caps, they move as a solid mass, their voices raised in fervor. The air is thick with tension as they wave the striking orange flags of Maulana's party, *Riyasat-e-Madina*.

The road is a blur of motion and sound, filled with the rhythmic chants and the bright flutter of flags, as the crowd presses forward, exuding an unmistakable aura of menace, defiance, and chants—'हम क्या चाहते?.....आज़ादी। चीन के लेंगे।.....आज़ादी। तेरा मेरा रिश्ता क्या?.....ला इलाह इल्लिल्लाह।....एक रूपए में दो मियाज़ि। .....गो नियाज़ी ..... गो नियाज़ि।' *(What we want? Freedom. Freedom. Go Niyazi. Go Niyazi.)*

Perched atop a container, Maulana delivers a fiery, high-voltage speech to the roaring crowd below. His words crackle with intensity, reverberating through the air, igniting the emotions of his illiterate and brainwashed followers. Their eyes are fixed on him, hanging onto every phrase, every gesture, as if each syllable were a decree. The crowd swells and surges in response, their chants rising in a chaotic symphony of blind devotion, their orange flags fluttering wildly as Maulana's voice booms over the Grand Trunk Road, commanding absolute attention.

'मैं आपके जस्बे हुब्बुल वतनि को सलाम करता हूँ। मैं आपके इस दिने इस्लाम के साथ मोहब्बत को सलाम करता हूँ। मैं इस मुल्क की नाजायज़ हुकूमत के खात्मे के लिए आपके पुरदोश होने को सलाम करता हूँ। जिस तरह मुझे अपने कारकूनो का खून अज़ीज़ है। जिस तरह मुझे अपने कारकूनो की ज़िन्दगी अज़ीज़

है। उसी तरह मुझे पाकिस्तान की पुलिस ,पाकिस्तान के रेंजर्स और पाकिस्तान के फ़ौज का खून भी अज़ीज़ है। इसीलिए बिना कोई जोर जबरदस्ती किये हम पाकिस्तान को इस सिलेक्टेड वज़ीर इ आज़म के चंगुल से बचाना चाहते है।' said Maulana.

I salute your passion for the country. I salute your faith in Islam. I salute your resistance against this government. The way in which I care for every drop of blood of my party workers in the same way I care for every drop of blood of my Pakistani police, rangers and army. That is why we will continue our march in a nonviolent way.

'एक रूपए में दो मियाज़ी, गो मियाज़ी गो मियाज़ी , क रूपए में दो मियाज़ी, गो मियाज़ी गो मियाज़ी। हिंदुस्तान जो यार है , गद्दार है गद्दार है।' roared the crowd. *Two Miyazis for one rupee. Go Miyazi. Go Miyazi. The one who is friend of India is a traitor.*

Local police and ISI officers are walking in the crowd in civilian dress, hoping to meet the Indian Kafirs.

***

Bara Market.

Rawalpindi. Pakistan.

At the same moment, a rickshaw weaves its way into Bara Market, Rawalpindi. Wrapped tightly in a gray shawl, Sambha, disguised as a rickshaw driver, blends seamlessly into the bustling crowd. The commercial street stretches long and dense with activity, teeming with vendors and shoppers. Armed police constables stand watch every hundred meters, some gripping assault rifles, others holding fiber sticks, their eyes scanning the crowd for any sign of trouble.

Sambha maintains a steady pace, his face obscured by the shawl, exuding the calm of just another driver on his daily route. The rickshaw comes to a gentle stop in front of a modest shop named *Bilal Toy Shop*. It's a small, unassuming place tucked between larger storefronts, its sign barely noticeable amidst the clutter of the street.

Sambha steps out, lifting a carton from the backseat of the rickshaw. He pushes through the shop's entrance.

'सलाम वालेकुम। आपका हि इंतज़ार कर रहा था। आओ बैठो।' said Haji Bilal Raza, rotating the beads between his fingers. *I was waiting for you. Please have a seat.*

Haji Bilal, a fifty-year-old, clean-shaven Islamic scholar, sits behind the counter. His movements are unhurried, deliberate, as if time itself bends to his will. As the president of the Bara Shop Owners Association, Haji Bilal is known for his methodical nature. Everything about him seems excruciatingly slow—his speech, his gestures—everything except the sharpness of his mind, which operates at a speed few can match.

Without a word, he reaches into a drawer, his hand emerging with a satellite phone. His eyes briefly meet Sambha's before he extends it toward him with the same measured calm. Sambha takes it, acknowledging the silent understanding that passes between them. No words are exchanged; none are needed.

'सिम कार्ड नया है। बोहोत टाइम लग जायेगा पुलिस को ट्रेस करने में।' said Haji Bilal. *SIM card is new. It will take some time to trace.*

'आप आये कियू नहीं?' asked Sambha. *Why didn't you come?*

'आप देख ही रहे है चरों तरफ घेरा लगा है। थोड़ा वक़्त लगा मुझे निकलने में. मै आया तबतक आप निकल चुके थे।' said Bilal. *You see all these police around. I took some time. But still, I came. But nobody was there.*

'उनके पास तुम्हारी फोटो भी है। ये देखो,' said Haji Bilal, showing Sambha his photo taken from CCTV footage of Chaudhary Guest House. *They have your photo. See this.*

'फिर मुझे यहाँ पकड़ा क्यों नहीं?' asked Sambha. *Then why didn't they catch me here.*

'आपने फ़ोन बंद किया हुआ है. कहाँ से पकड़ेंगे आपको।' said Bilal. *You have switched off your phone. How can they catch you?*

'इंटेल क्या है?' asked Sambha. *What is the intel?*

'सारा GT रोड रेंजर्स से भरा हुआ है. वहां से जाना मुनासिब नहीं होगा।' said Haji Bilal. Grand Trunk Road is full of rangers in civil uniform. It is not feasible to go from there.

'मौलाना क्या कर रहा है?' asked Sambha. *What Maulana is doing?*

'फ़ौज से बात हो रही है जनाब।' said Haji Bilal. *He is talking to army.*

'तुम्ही ने सारा कम्युनिकेशन हैक करवाया ना?' asked Sambha. *Are you the one behind the breach in communication?*

Sambha pulls out his pistol with a suppressor and points at Haji Bilal.

'क़ुरान-ए-पाक की कसम साहब. सच बोल रहा हूँ,' said Haji Bilal. *Swear on Quran. I am not lying.*

يَٰٓأَيُّهَا ٱلَّذِينَ ءَامَنُوا لَا تَتَّخِذُوا ٱلْيَهُودَ وَٱلنَّصَٰرَىٰٓ أَوْلِيَآءَ بَعْضُهُمْ أَوْلِيَآءُ بَعْضٍ وَمَن يَتَوَلَّهُم مِّنكُمْ فَإِنَّهُۥ مِنْهُمْ إِنَّ ٱللَّهَ لَا يَهْدِى ٱلْقَوْمَ ٱلظَّٰلِمِين ٥١,' recites Sambha and shoots Bilal.

O you who believe! Do not take the Jews and the Christians as allies—some of them are allies of one another. Whoever of you allies himself with them is one of them. Allah does not guide the wrongdoing people. Surah al-Maidah 51.

Bilal falls, splashing the blood on the backside wall.

Sambha tucks the pistol back into his thigh holster, grabs one of the top cartons, and strides out of the shop. He pulls down the rolling shutter, glancing around cautiously. Armed police officers are scattered throughout the busy street, their watchful eyes surveying the market. Remaining calm, Sambha grabs a dirty, crumpled sheet from the rickshaw and wraps it around his shoulders. Then, he picks up a filthy sack and slings it over his shoulder, turning into a ragpicker.

Leaving the rickshaw behind, he slips into a narrow alley beside Bilal Toy Shop. The passage is dim and claustrophobic, and as he ventures deeper, two armed rangers suddenly appear at the far end, heading straight toward him. Heart racing, Sambha glances around desperately. With no way to retreat, he spots a filthy, half-broken door hanging ajar. He shoves it open and slips inside.

The stench hits him immediately—a thick, nauseating odor that clings to the air. He stands in the dark, decrepit confines of a public toilet, its walls smeared and discolored with grime. There's no light, only the faint outline of corners piled high with trash: rotting garbage, used syringes, needles, crumpled silver foils, used condoms, and stained sanitary pads. It's a place abandoned by time and humanity, the smell so suffocating it reminds him of a neglected morgue.

Like an unconscious drug addict he lay in the garbage, wedging his head between his knees.

Two rangers enter the toilet. They ignore the drug edict.

'भाई कब तक तैनाती है हमारी यहाँ इस बरा बजार में?' said ranger, urinating. *How long we are going to be here in this Bara Market?*

'पता नहीं भाई। खुद कुश हमलावर की तलाश में है ये लोग शायद,' said another ranger, urinating. *I don't know brother. They lookout for some suicide bomber, I think.*

'मेरे करीबी रिश्तेदार को खोया है मैंने मुल्तान के ब्लास्ट में। अल्लाह करे वो हमलावर यहाँ ना हो।' said ranger. *I lost my relative in Multan blast. I pray that suicide bombers are not here.*

Rangers walk out. After a moment Sambha also walk out in opposite direction.

Sambha crouched low, pretending to rummage through the heaps of refuse piled in front of the Akbar Building at the heart of Bara Market. His eyes darted around. The entire area was swarming with rangers and police, their presence suffocating. Armed men stood guard near every corner, and the road leading to the main entrance of the market was choked with an anxious crowd.

Realizing escape would be nearly impossible from ground level, Sambha made a quick decision. He needed a bird's-eye view. He discreetly set his plastic bag in a corner, blending in with the filth around him, and slipped into the entrance of the old Akbar Building. He began climbing the worn, creaky stairs.

By the time he reached the third floor, a sudden shout echoed down the corridor.

'रुक जा,' said a ranger who was climbing down. *Stop.*

Sambha stop.

'ज ज जनाब क क क चरा. देख र र र हा. हूँ,' stuttered Sambha. *I am checking garbage.*

'आज नहीं। कल आओ। निचे उतरो ।' said the ranger. *Not now. Do it tomorrow. Go.*

Sambha remains perfectly still, eyes narrowed as the ranger closes in, his boots thudding softly against the floorboards. Then, in a blur of motion, Sambha springs into action. Three swift, precise strikes—a chop to the neck, a jab to the ribs, and a final elbow to the temple—send the ranger crumpling to the ground, unconscious but alive.

Without a moment's hesitation, Sambha draws his pistol, the suppressor glinting faintly in the dim light. A single, muffled shot. The ranger's body jolts briefly, then goes still.

'ह ह ह हर हर महादेव,' whispered Sambha. *H H H Har Har Mahadev.*

Sambha dumps the ranger's body into the plastic drum and moves on.

On the terrace, Sambha spots a sniper positioning his rifle toward the main gate of Bara Market. Without hesitation, Sambha takes aim and fires a clean headshot from behind. The sniper collapses instantly, dead. But as Sambha scans the surroundings, he notices another sniper perched on the terrace of the building across the street.

Down below, the situation is tightening—police officers have begun meticulous man-to-man checks, stopping every vehicle that passes. Sambha's gaze shifts to the back of the building, where he sees a glimpse of the highway beyond the maze of shops and structures.

With no time to waste, Sambha turns and bolts, sprinting across the rooftop. He maneuvers through the tangled mess of electric wires, leaping and climbing with agility. He jumps from one roof to the next, running across the tops of the buildings, a shadow moving silently through the chaotic labyrinth of the market below.

'जनाब नगीना के छत पे मूवमेंट है।' said the spinner, on his hands-free. *Sir, there is movement on the roof of Nagina market.*

A sniper's scope catches a glimpse of movement—Sambha darting across the rooftops. Instantly, the sniper's crosshairs lock onto his silhouette. He steadies his aim, finger tightening on the trigger, ready to take the shot.

'पक्का वही है?' asked Fawad, who is present in the market and leading the operation. *Are you sure it's him?*

'पक्का नहीं है सर।' said the snipper. *No Sir, I am not sure.*

'कोई शहरी मरना नहीं चाहिए. वर्ना यहाँ फसाद हो जाएगा। तुम नज़र रखो मैं लड़के भेजता हूँ।' said Fawad. *No civilian casualty. It will be a riot situation here. You keep looking at him and inform me as soon as, you are sure. I am sending the boys.*

'जी जनाब।' said the snipper, sighting at Sambha's back, through the scope. *Yes, Sir.*

Fawad gets one more call. This time it's a ranger.

'जनाब एक रेंजर को गोली लगी है. वो शहीद हो गया है।' said the ranger. *Sir, the ranger is shot. He is dead.*

'कहाँ?' asked Fawad. *Where?*

'अकबर बिल्डिंग में दूसरे मंज़िल पर।' said the ranger. *Here on the second floor of Akhbar Building.*

'तुम चौकन्ना रहो।' said Fawad. *You stay alert.*

Fawad makes a call to snipper.

'गोली चला दो,' said Fawad to the snipper. *Take the shot.*

'ठीक है,' said the snipper, taking a long breath. *Yes, Sir.*

But Sambha is already ahead of him, staying low and weaving through the cluttered rooftop—ducking behind concrete columns, slipping past water tanks, and crouching beside metal scraps and parapet walls. He moves like a ghost, blending seamlessly into the chaotic terrain, making it nearly impossible for the sniper to get a clear shot.

Sambha takes a chance and cranes his head out cautiously from behind a water tank. His eyes narrow as he spots rangers swarming around the base of the Nagina Building, tightening their perimeter. The number of armed men encircling the structure is daunting—each one scanning for any sign of movement. CLACK. A bullet whistles past Sambha's head, grazing his hair before slamming into a plastic water drum. Water starts trickling out, pooling on the rooftop. Sambha drops flat behind a small concrete parapet, his breathing controlled.

He reaches for a shard of broken mirror and tilts it just enough to catch a glimpse of the sniper. The sniper, steady as stone, exhales slowly, his rifle poised, waiting for Sambha to expose himself. Sambha studies him, timing each breath. He knows the critical moment—the gap between exhale and inhale. As soon as the sniper slightly shifts his head to readjust, Sambha seizes the opportunity. He darts to the edge of the backside roof, slipping out of the sniper's line of sight and into a shadowed ginnel below.

Swiftly, Sambha sheds the blanket and crouches, bracing his palms firmly on the roof's edge. In one fluid motion, he lowers his body, releasing his grip to land softly on a narrow concrete window ledge below. He doesn't pause. With a light jump, he drops to the roof of a smaller adjacent building. Moving like a cat, Sambha spreads his arms and legs, wedging himself tightly between two parallel walls, and begins a careful descent.

Halfway down, a ranger unexpectedly steps into the ginnel below, his eyes widening in shock. As he raises his AK47, aiming squarely at Sambha, the sound of a single suppressed shot from Sambha's pistol cuts through the silence—*THUMP*. The ranger crumples instantly, the rifle slipping from his grasp. Dead.

Sambha jumps the remaining distance, rolling onto his shoulder and landing in a heap of garbage. He rises quickly, brushing off the grime, and pulls out his satellite phone. With a quick tap, he powers it on, fully aware of the risk of being tracked. Time is short, and every second the device is active could draw unwanted eyes to his location. Sambha stays low, lying besides the dead ranger.

***

ISI Control Room.

Rawalpindi. Pakistan.

An alert starts flashing on the video wall. Hamid makes a call to Fawad.

'संभा वहीँ आसपास है। कन्फर्म। मै स्पेशल फोर्स भेज रहा हूँ।' said Hamid on the phone. *It's confirmed that Sambha is in the Bara Market area. I am sending special forces.*

'जी जनाब,' said Fawad, on the phone. *Yes, Sir.*

***

Bara Market.

Rawalpindi. Pakistan.

The dead ranger's phone rings. Sambha takes out the phone from the ranger's pocket.

'जनाब।' answered Sambha, in different voice. *Yes. Sir.*

'वो यहीं हमारे आसपास है। अगर दिखे तो सीधा गोली मर देना। पूछने की जरुरत नहीं है,' said Fawad, on phone. *He is nearby. If you see him, you shoot him directly. Don't wait for the permission.*

'जनाब।' *answered Sambha. Yes. Sir.*

Sambha's suspicions about Bilal were confirmed—Bilal had betrayed him. Without a second thought, Sambha breaks into a sprint, weaving through the narrow alleys and heading straight for the highway.

***

Iqbal Road. Bara Market.

Rawalpindi.

Sambha slips out of the market, seamlessly merging into the bustling crowd on Iqbal Road. Keeping his head low and movements casual, he scans his surroundings, alert for any sign of pursuit.

Just then, a truck catches his eye—a hulking vehicle revving up to leave, the driver impatiently honking and turning the wheels toward the main road. He takes a long drag from his beedi, blowing out a cloud of smoke as he casually saunters closer. With a quick glance over his shoulder, Sambha peeks into the trolley hitched to the truck. It's empty.

Making his move, Sambha discreetly slips his satellite phone into a corner of the trolley and steps back, blending into the crowd once more. Without a pause, he crosses the street and ducks into a crowded tea stall on the opposite side of Iqbal Road. Settling into the corner, he pulls his shawl tighter around his shoulders, his eyes trained on the truck as it lumbers onto the highway. Now, anyone tracking the signal will be chasing a ghost.

'एक चाय देना,' said Sambha to the vendor. *Tea please.*

Fawad's Jeep screeches to a halt in front of the tea stall across Iqbal Road. He steps out, followed by the rangers, their eyes scanning the crowded street. The locals barely glance up—scenes like this are routine here.

Sambha sits motionless in the corner of the tea stall, his posture relaxed as he sips his tea. His face is a mask of calm, blending seamlessly with the chaos around him. Only his eyes follow the movements of the rangers, tracking their every step.

The truck rumbles away, disappearing into the traffic. Fawad's gaze lingers momentarily in the direction of its retreating taillights, suspicion etched across his face. Just then, his phone rings, moving the attention.

'Yes,' answered Fawad.

'वो तेजी से भाग रहा है। हाईवे पर है। मशरिक़ की ओर।' said, the operator, on phone. *He is going away fast. He is on the highway towards east.*

'OK,' said Fawad, keeping his phone down.

'चलो,' shouts Fawad, jumping in the Jeep. *Let's go.*

The rangers scramble into the Jeep, slamming the doors shut. The Jeep lunges forward, tires screeching as it tears down the road, speeding off in the direction the truck had taken.

Sambha discreetly places a few notes on the tea stall counter and slips away, maneuvering through the crowd. He squeezes into an overcrowded minibus, pushing his way past tightly packed passengers, his small frame vanishing amidst the crush of bodies.

The minibus rattles through the bustling streets, and as it nears Committee Chowk Metro Station, Sambha jumps off. He glances around briefly, then heads toward the shadowed area under the flyover, where his police van is concealed. Sliding into the driver's seat, he starts the engine and pulls away smoothly, blending effortlessly into the flow of traffic.

***

Grand Trunk Road.

Pakistan.

Tension on GT Road has spiraled into chaos. Anger among the Riyasat-e-Madina Party workers is boiling over, fueled by the relentless police checks.

The air is thick with aggression as furious chants rise against the authorities. News of Bilal's brutal murder has spread like wildfire, igniting the crowd further. Abuses are hurled at the army, and clashes with the police have already broken out. In a violent show of rage, two police vans have been set ablaze, the flames licking the sky as smoke billows upward.

'लब्बैक लब्बैक लब्बैक या रसूल अल्लाह,' chants workers. *Labbaik labbaik labbaik ya rasool allah.*

***

Bilal Toy Shop.

Bara Market.

Rawalpindi.

In front of Bilal Toy Shop, a dense crowd of furious shopkeepers has gathered around Bilal's dead body, their faces twisted with grief and anger. Voices rise in a chorus of outrage, echoing through the narrow market streets. The shopkeepers, holding up makeshift signs and shouting slogans, are united in their protest against what they perceive as yet another act of police brutality.

'हम आपको लाश नहीं ले जाने देंगे। पहले बताना होगा की उसको किसने मारा।' said one of the protesters. *We will not allow you to take the body. First you have to tell us who kill him.*

The police are struggling to contain and negotiate with the enraged protesters.

***

Ganj Mandi Road.

Rawalpindi.

Angry Fawad is interrogating the truck driver.

'देख चुपचाप बता कहाँ और कौन है तेरे साथ? कहाँ जा रहा था तू. देख गोली मार दूंगा।' asked Fawad. *Where are going? Who else is there with you? Tell me fast. Otherwise, I will shoot you.*

'गरीब आदमी हूँ. साहब ये अंडे की ट्रक है. पोल्ट्री जा रहा था तो अपने रोक लिया।' siad truck driver. *I am a poor man. I was going to poultry to load the truck.*

'अबे तो क्या कण्ट्रोल रूम वाले पागल है क्या?' said Fawad. *You think people sitting in control room are mad?*

'मुझे क्या मालूम साहब।' said truck driver. *How can I know Sir.*

***

Dates Godown.

Muzaffarabad.

It's one in the afternoon when Sambha arrives at the abandoned godown on the outskirts of Muzaffarabad. The high-ceiling warehouse is packed with towering stacks of date sacks, casting long shadows across the dusty floor. In the center, a carbon fiber coffin-like box rests with Bharat lying inside. His eyes flutter open, slowly regaining some consciousness.

'धन्यवाद मित्रा,' said Bharat to Sambha. *Thanks, buddy.*

'झालं आता. थोडंसच ऱ्हायलं,' said Sambha. *Don't worry. We are going back. Just a couple of hours more.*

Bharat smiles.

'चल,' said Sambha, to Sarah. *Get ready.*

'Yes. Sir,' replied Sarah.

Sarah dragas the cover tightly over the coffin-like box and secures it with locks. The box is sealed, save for two ventilation pipes that provide airflow. Sambha and Sarah begin loading the remaining sacks of dates into the truck, stacking them carefully around and over the hidden box.

Once the cargo is in place, Sambha adjusts a black-and-white checkered scarf around his head, pulling it low to obscure his face. He strides to the front and climbs into the driver's seat. The vehicle is a brightly adorned Mazda Hino 7D, its body covered in vibrant red floral patterns and intricate calligraphy, while colorful chains dangle from the bumpers. Sambha steers the truck out of the godown.

Meanwhile, Sarah, dressed in a silk burqa, her face hidden behind sunglasses and a gold watch glinting on her wrist, eases the black Toyota Yaris out of the gowdown, smoothly in the opposite direction.

***

Sarah's House.

India.

'नानि जेवन खरंच मस्त आहे इथे. नॉन वेज. आनि सगळ्यात छान म्हनजे इथली डिलिव्हरी . बरोबर टायमाला आनतात आपली ऑर्डर,' said Sarah who is sitting in her cabin in Indian Embassy, Islamabad, to her Nanny, on the phone. *The food is really good here. The best part is the delivery. It's never late.*

'चला म्हनजे काहीतरी आहे जे तुला आवडतंय,' said, Nanny. *Thank God. At least there is something that you liked.*

From this conversation, Patil seated beside Nanny gets the clear message from Sarah about the progress and safety of the plan. Nodding to Nanny, he gets up and walks out of the house. Nanny and Sahara continue their chat.

***

Warehouse.

Muzaffarabad.

At two in the afternoon, a long line of trucks snakes through the premises of the government warehouse in Langarpura, Muzaffarabad. Drivers stand patiently beside their vehicles, clutching stacks of papers, waiting for their turn at the clearance counter. Trading officers sit at their desks, meticulously checking and stamping each file before allowing the goods to proceed toward the border.

However, every driver knows the unwritten rule: five-thousand-rupee notes must be discreetly tucked inside the paperwork. It's not considered a bribe, just a gesture of appreciation that keeps the process smooth and efficient.

Being his first day on the job, Sambha took no chances. He slipped in fifteen thousand rupees under his clearance file—five thousand as a thank-you and an additional ten thousand for securing a coveted special driving license, issued only to drivers operating on the India-Pakistan border route. It doesn't matter that his papers are all forged.

With his papers stamped and the transaction complete, Sambha steps out of the office.

***

Grand Trunk Road.

Pakistan.

One party worker is dead, and several others are injured from police firing. The situation is spiraling out of control, with chaos spreading rapidly. News channels are sensationalizing the incident, fueling anger and confusion. The entire narrative is unraveling, and amidst the escalating mayhem, no one seems to have a clear grasp of the situation—not even Hakimullah.

***

Jamia Naeemia Madrasa.

Lahore. Pakistan.

Hakimullah is watching the riots − vehicles burning, police firing, tear gas, injuries, deaths.

His phone rings. It's Sheikh Zafar Abbas from Dubai.

'ما الذي يجري؟,' asked Hakimullah. *What is going on?*

'إنه مجرد عمل كالمعتاد,' said Sheik. *It's just a business as usual.*

'هل هو مرتبط بـ RAW,' asked Hakimullah. *Is it related to RAW?*

'أنا لا أعتقد ذلك,' said Sheikh. *I don't think so.*

'إذن لماذا يشتعل مولانا؟ لماذا انشغل الجميع في روالبندي فجأة؟,' asked Hakimullah. *Then why Maulana is on fire? Why everybody in Rawalpindi suddenly got busy?*

'أعتقد أن لدي شيء لك,' said Sheikh. *I think I have something for you.*

'ماذا؟,' asked Hakimullah. *What?*

'ماهو الإتفاق؟,' asked Sheikh. *What is the deal?*

'ما تريد؟,' asked Hakimullah. *What you want?*

'مليون دولار. في حساب التشفير الخاص بي. الآن,' said Sheikh. *One million dollars. In my crypto account. Right now.*

'ما هذا؟,' asked Hakimullah. *What is it?*

'الساعة تدق. الوقت يمضي,' said Sheikh. *Clock is ticking. Time is running.*

Hakimullah completes the money transfer. Moments later, Sheikh sends him a photograph featuring himself, Shahbaz Sharif, and Mohammad, all standing together.

Unbeknownst to him, Hakimullah's phone is under surveillance. The image doesn't just land in his inbox—it also pings directly to General Hamid.

***

Space Orbit.

The Pakistani satellite is changing its direction. Changing its coordinates.

***

Trade Center.

Chakothi. Pakistan.

It took Sambha an hour to reach the Line of Control (LOC) Checkpoint and Trade Center at Chakothi. The time is now four in the afternoon. Armed security personnel stand watch, their eyes sharp and vigilant, monitoring every movement as a long line of trucks inches toward the gate.

Two trucks have already cleared the scanning machine, slowly rolling across the border into India.

Sambha's truck is next in line. He grips the steering wheel tightly, maintaining a calm demeanor as the guards gesture him forward. His truck rumbles toward the scanner, its red floral patterns glinting under the harsh afternoon light.

***

Space Orbit.

The Indian satellite is changing its orientation. Changing its coordinates.

***

Bahirji Complex.

India.

Infobeam's Master Control Panel appears on the video wall of Bahirji Complex. Green dots start appearing around the Chakothi region.

'सर चकोठी टर्मिनल कनेक्ट झालंय,' said the operator. *Sir we are connected to Chakothi terminal.*

'Good,' said Patil.

'सर एक्सपोस होन्याची शक्यता आहे . किती वेळ ठेऊ कनेकशन?' said the operator. *How long do you want me to keep the connection. It might get exposed.*

'राहू दे. संभा पोहोचत असेल,' said Patil. *Keep it. Sambha will be reaching the scanner at any moment now.*

The operator takes the order and starts typing the code. There is dead silence in the room except for the keyboard sound.

The operator receives the command and immediately begins typing the code. The only sound in the room is the clacking of the keyboard, cutting through the tense silence. Everyone holds their breath, eyes fixed on the screen, waiting for the outcome.

***

Home Minister House.

Islamabad. Pakistan.

General Hamid has gone mad over the Home Minister of Pakistan, Shahbaz Sharif.

General Hamid is seething with rage at Pakistan's Home Minister, Shahbaz Sharif. His face is flushed, eyes blazing as he paces back and forth, fists clenched in barely contained fury.

'वज़ीर साहब क्या डील है?' said Hamid, showing the photo of Mohammad. *What is the deal, Mr. Minister? Who is this man? Please tell me fast. I don't have time.*

'किसी पार्टी में मिला होगा बस। मुझे तो नाम भी नहीं पता उसका।' said Shahbaz Sharif. *I must have met him in some party. I don't even remember his name.*

Hamid loses his control. He gives a tight slap on the Minister's face.

'मेरे पास इतना वक्त नहीं है। आप खलीफा मत बनो। मैं तुमको यहीं मार दूंगा तुम्हारे घर में।' said Hamid *I don't have time. Don't be khalifa. I swear I will kill you right here in your house.*

'एक छोटासा टेंडर अलॉट किया है. बस और कुछ नहीं,' said Shahbaz. *It's about a small IT contract and nothing else.*

'कौनसी कंपनी है?' asked Hamid. *What is the company name?*

'इन्फोबिम,' said Shahbaz. *Infobeam.*

'सभी बॉर्डर क्लोज करो। पहले तोरखम,चकोटि और वाघा करो।' said Hamid to his assistant standing beside him. *Close all the borders. Stop the movement on Tokham, Chakothi, and Wagha.*

'जी जनाब,' said the assistant, taking out the phone. *Yes Sir.*

'क्या कोई बात हो गयी है?' asked Shahbaz. *Any problem?*

'अब तुम चुपचाप लन्दन निकल जाओ. वर्ना जेल में सड़ने के लिए तैयार हो जाओ।' said Hamid and walked away.

***

Trade Center.

Chakothi. Pakistan.

Sambha eases the truck forward, inching it carefully through the towering iron frame of the transmission X-ray machine.

Miles away, at the Bahirji Complex, the master console instantly updates, reflecting the results from the scanning console at Chakothi. All ten indicator lights blink green—no irregularities detected. The Chakothi operator presses the print command. The printer whirs softly, producing a hard copy of the results. She stamps and signs the document before handing it over to the waiting guard. He nods, then approaches Sambha, passing him the stamped results through the driver's window. Sambha accepts the papers with a smile, tucking them away securely.

'शुक्रिया जनाब,' said Sambha. *Thank you, Sir.*

Sambha takes the truck ahead.

***

Bahirji Complex.

India.

The control room is gripped by a tense, suffocating silence. Every heartbeat seems to have paused as all eyes remain glued to the screen, tracking the tiny dot representing Sambha's truck. No one moves, no one breathes—the anticipation is electric. They wait, nerves stretched taut, for that crucial moment when Sambha's truck crosses over and finally touches Indian soil.

***

LOC Crossing.

Chakothi. Pakistan.

With only half an hour left until the LOC trade closes at five, the trucks inch forward at a painfully slow pace. The minutes seem to stretch endlessly as the convoy crawls along. Up ahead, the high concrete entrance arch looms, its signboard reading: *Salambad 2 KM.*

Sambha keeps his gaze steady as the long-awaited sight begins to come into view. Indian Army guards stand vigilant on either side of the road, their uniforms crisp against the fading daylight. And then he sees it—the Indian tricolor, flurrying proudly in the breeze.

His breath catches. His eyes widen, sparkling with emotion. It's a sight he's longed to see, and now, as he rolls slowly forward, the border just a few meters away, Sambha's eyes glisten, unable to contain the wave of pride and relief washing over him.

***

Cargo Hall.

Uri. India

Sambha's truck rumbles into the Cargo Hall at Salambad, Uri, India, just minutes before the closing hour. Clearing the first round of manual security checks, it rolls forward into the gantry X-ray scanning system.

Inside the operator's room, eyes are fixed on the screen. The thermal scan of Sambha's truck gradually appears on the monitor. A red horizontal line glows sharply across the middle of the trolley, standing out against the rest of the image. Alarmed, the operator's pulse quickens. He hits the print button, tearing off the sheet and rushing out of the room.

He bursts into the supervisor's cabin, holding the printout. Meanwhile, Sambha remains in the truck, waiting.

'सर मानसाचं किंवा जनावरांचं शरीर दिसतंय,' said the operator, showing the printout. *Sir, it's an animal or a human body.*

Sandeep Kaul is present in the supervisor's cabin.

'रिमार्क मध्ये 'माझ्या कडून स्पेशल परवानगी'असं लिही,' said the supervisor. *Write 'Specially approved by me' in the remarks. And clear the Truck. Very Quickly.*

'ठीक आहे सर,' said the operator, walking out of the cabin. *OK Sir.*

Finally, an Indian guard approaches Sambha's truck, handing over the clearance papers through the open driver's window.

'शुक्रिया जनाब,' said Sambha. *Shukriya Janab.*

***

Cargo Hall Parking.

Uri. India.

The final barricade lifts, and the truck rolls into the parking area of the Cargo Hall in Salambad, Uri. As soon as Sambha steps out of the vehicle, a flurry of activity erupts around him. Government officials, security personnel, and a team of doctors, already poised for action, surrounding the truck.

'छत्रपति शिवजी महाराज की जय।' whispers Sambha, touching his forehead on the motherland. *Chatrapati Shivaji Maharaj Ki Jai'*

Sambha gets up and starts walking with government officials waiting for him. With no permission to share his story, Sambha remains disguised as a Pakistani truck driver and follows the group of government officials.

***

Air India Flight.
Indian Airspace.

Sarah is finally returning to the motherland. Seated by the window, she gazes out at the vast expanse of sky. Her heart is filled with unspoken prayers and quiet anticipation.

***

Mahadev Temple.
Pimpri. India.

Patil is standing among the crowd, attending the evening *aarti* in the beautiful riverside old Mahadev Temple at Pimple Saudagar.

***

Sambha House.
India.

Bharat is on the mend, his strength slowly returning. Though the plaster will need to stay on for a while longer, his condition is improving every day. Meanwhile, Gauri busies herself in the kitchen, preparing lunch for her brother.

***

Sahyadri Mountain Range.

Pune. India.

'महाराssssssज

गडपती

गजअश्वपती

भूपती

प्रजापती

सुवर्णरत्नश्रीपती

अष्टवधानजागृत

अष्टप्रधानवेष्टित

न्यायालंकारमंडित

शस्त्रास्त्रशास्त्रपारंगत

राजनितिधुरंधर

प्रौढप्रतापपुरंदर

क्षत्रियकुलावतंस

सिंहासनाधिश्वर

श्री श्रीमंत महाराजाधिराज

छत्रपती महाराजांचा,' sang Sambha, standing on the ridge, under the cool golden light of the rising sun.

'विजय असो,' shouted Sarah and new recruits, standing in the line on the ridge. The roar of *Shivgarjana* echoes all around the Sahyadri Mountain Range.